CANCELLED

A Bowl of Sun

"It's time that child was sent to school," the customer's voice said briskly. "You know you can't keep her with you forever, Mike."

Megan held her breath. She waited for Mike to reply.

"I know," she heard Mike say, "but the kind of school she needs is not close by. I didn't want to send her away too soon."

Send her away! Megan almost laughed out loud. Mike would never send her away. She knew that. They were buddies. Mike needed her. He was joking with the customer, of course, just the way he always did.

Even so, she could feel a small, cold knot of fear deep inside her. She pretended it was not there, but it did not go away.

For a long time Megan had not even known that she was blind. Outside the house, Mike's firm, strong hand had taught her how to move from here to there, from this place to that. Inside the house she knew just where everything was. She could easily find her way alone from her own small room with its soft bed, through the living room, and on out to the front where Mike had his shop.

Mike was her father. He worked very hard cutting and stitching his fine new leather. From the leather he made belts, sandals, and bags. These he sold in his shop. The new leather was smooth and smelled better than almost anything.

"The leather is brown as chocolate," Mike told Megan. "With a sharp knife it cuts like butter."

Megan liked being near Mike as he worked. She kept the shop tidy, sweeping up the scraps of leather that fell to the floor. She made sandwiches for lunch, and they ate them when there were no customers.

"Is this your little girl?" people would often ask Mike.

"We are buddies," Mike would laugh in reply. "Together we stand, divided we fall!"

When business was good Mike worked all day and most of the night. "We can't afford to run short of things to sell when we have many customers," he would say. "During the slow seasons I can catch up on my rest."

Before Megan went to bed she always made two big mugs of cocoa. She put them carefully on a tray, together with a plate of cookies. Then she would carry the tray slowly into Mike's shop. She knew every step of the way.

Everything would seem very quiet after the busy day. They talked about the shop, the customers, and the things Mike was planning to make next.

When business was bad, and on Sunday afternoons, they walked down to the seashore. It was only a short walk to the water.

Hand in hand, Mike and Megan made tracks with their bare feet in the wet sand by the edge of the sea.

"Nobody lives a better life than we do," said Mike. He squeezed Megan's hand with pleasure.

Megan nodded. She was sure that nobody did.

The cold water slid over their bare feet, and then away. Patches of silky soft foam clung to their ankles. Megan scooped big handfuls of the fine sand. She parted her fingers slowly, feeling the sand trickle through in a thin stream. Together they built a wonderful sand castle with great tall towers and bridges and moats. Then they waited while the tide moved slowly up onto the shore and finally washed it all away.

A long time ago Mike had told her about castles. He had held Megan's hand in his, moving it over the sand. He helped her mold the wet sand until she had learned to make the shapes he told her about.

Megan stroked and patted the cool, damp sides of the castle until they were nearly as smooth as Mike's leather.

"The sun will soon be gone," Mike said as last. "It is time to go home. The sky is getting pink."

"Really pink?" Megan wanted to know.

"Pink as a rose," Mike replied.

Megan smiled. She knew that pink was a happy color. The sound of Mike's voice told her that. She remembered the smell of a rose. It must be a very happy sky, she thought. She put her hand in Mike's and they started for home.

Every night Megan went to sleep listening to the sound of the waves washing up onto the sand. When it stormed, she curled under the warm covers and listened to the pounding thunder of waves and the lonesome moan of the fog horn. It was wild and wonderful, and she knew that Mike was nearby.

Mike and Megan lived in a small, friendly town. All day long people dropped into the shop to chat with Mike. They sat on benches and watched him cut and stitch. Almost everyone in town wore sandals that Mike had made.

Megan knew who most of the children in town were. She could hear them shouting and playing all day. Sometimes they came into the shop to watch, too. But most of the time the children had games to play or places to go.

One evening after Mike had closed the shop, he arranged his tools neatly and lined up some of the new sandals in the long, glass case.

"Next week is your birthday," he told Megan as they closed the door to the shop. "I was thinking it might be nice to have a party."

Megan caught her breath. "Did you say a party?" she asked in surprise. She thought there must be some mistake. They had never had a party. She had never even thought of having one. It had always been just the two of them—she and Mike together.

Megan hung her head. Usually whatever Mike wanted, she wanted, too. "I don't think I would like a party," she said in a small voice.

Mike said nothing for a moment. When he spoke again, he spoke in the kind of voice he used when he had made up his mind about something.

"It's time we thought of things like parties," he said. "We can't put off school much longer. You must learn to get along with other children."

Megan felt the strange fear growing again. She had Mike. She didn't need anyone else. The fear rose from the pit of her stomach and left a lump in her throat. Before she could stop them, tears were stinging her eyes. She wiped them away quickly. A buddy never cried. Mike never did.

"Anyway," Mike added, trying to be cheerful, "parties are meant to be fun. I never heard of anyone not wanting a party. If two old buddies like we are can't put together the best party of them all, then I say we don't deserve to have one!"

Megan laughed. There was nothing to be afraid of, she told herself. She could trust Mike. If he wanted a party, then she wanted one too.

To Megan's surprise, it turned out to be fun helping Mike get ready for the party. They blew up balloons and hung them from the ceiling. They hid peanuts everywhere for the children to find. Mike bought a pink cake with pink candles, and strawberry soda in tall bottles. Every child who had come into the shop the week before had been invited.

"They won't all come," Mike laughed. "If they did, I don't know what we would do with them!"

Megan laughed, too. Maybe nobody will come, she thought. Maybe Mike and I will have the party

all to ourselves—the balloons, the peanuts, and
even the pink cake with its pink candles.

Everybody came. They filled the shop. They
overflowed into the other rooms and out the back
door. They laughed and sang "Happy Birthday."
They shouted back and forth to their friends. They
climbed over things, and crawled under things
looking for peanuts. They burst balloons and
threw popcorn. They plunked a steady stream of
birthday presents on Megan's lap. They chattered
with one another and ate cake and drank
strawberry soda.

19

Then, just as suddenly as they had come, they were gone. Not even an echo of their merry voices was left. A hollow silence seemed to hang over the shop.

Megan could hear Mike's sandals crunching on peanut shells as he cleared away the fancy paper plates and wiped up puddles of strawberry soda from the floor. He picked up cake crumbs and scraps of burst balloons.

"Let's not have another party, Mike," Megan said at last.

Mike laughed. "There's nothing wrong with parties," he said. "It's just that we need a little practice, you and I."

After the party, for the first time in her life, Megan felt lonely. Mike felt something, too. He talked more than usual with the children who came into the shop. He asked them about school. He invited them to share their sandwiches at lunchtime. He gave them chores to do and praised their good work. He even asked some of them to come along when he and Megan walked by the sea on Sunday afternoons. It was almost never just the two of them as it had been before.

Then, suddenly, the rest of Megan's familiar world turned upside down. She heard Mike's voice trying its best to make her understand what was happening.

"We are going to move," he told her.

"Move?"

Megan had never thought of moving. She knew that there were other people and places, but they had never seemed quite real to her before.

"We are moving to Boston," Mike went on. "You will go to school. You know it cannot always be just the two of us. You must have a chance to learn to live your life in your own way."

There was a long pause when nobody said anything at all.

"You will learn to read," Mike said. "Reading is a way of knowing things. People need to know things."

Megan did not reply. She could think of nothing that she did not already know.

"In the school where you will go," Mike continued, "the children learn to read with their hands. People whose eyes cannot see need to have their hands trained to take the place of the eyes. There are not many schools like that, but there is one near Boston. That is why we have to move."

24

Before Megan knew what was happening, everything was arranged. Mike said he would work in a leather shop in Boston. He would make belts and sandals just as he had before. The new shop, he told Megan, would be a lot bigger than the one he had now. There would be more leather and more tools, and there would be other people to help. He and Megan would live in a big house that Mike had found close by the new shop. A lot of other people lived there too. "That way," Mike explained, "you will not be alone when I work late at the shop."

There was nothing Megan could do. Everything seemed to happen so fast. She felt lost in a whirl of packing boxes, moving vans, and good-byes. Her head spun. The things and the people she had always known seemed to melt away. The sound and smell of the ocean faded into the distance. Strange new sounds and smells crowded in to take their place.

The new world was one of hustle and bustle. The sounds were of traffic, sirens, and strange voices that never stopped. It was a world of unfamiliar spaces and strange objects.

Megan felt alone and helpless. She waited to be taken from this place to that, from her new home to her new school, and back again. She didn't try to do anything by herself.

Mike was worried and upset. "She has never been so helpless," he told Rose. Rose lived in a corner room in the big house. She made clay pots on a wheel to sell, and wove soft things on a big loom.

"It will take time," Rose told him. "It is a change that is not easy for her. She will learn to like us. You will see."

"Back home," Mike said sadly, "I would almost forget that she couldn't see. She did everything by herself. I thought she needed a school and other people. Could it be that I was wrong?"

"Don't worry," said Rose. "It will work out."

But things did not seem to be working out at all. Day after day, when Megan was brought from school, she sat alone by the open window remembering the smell of the sea. She heard the harsh sounds of a busy city and remembered the sound of the waves gently washing up onto the sand.

Sometimes Rose took her to Mike's shop. The smell of the leather was the same, but Mike did not need her now. Somebody else tidied the shop and swept up the scraps.

The teachers at the school shook their heads. "She is no trouble," they told Mike, "but she will not try anything by herself. You must do your best to help."

"Have Rose bring you down to the shop after school," Mike told Megan one morning. "We will go for a walk in the park when I am through working. We will go for a ride on the swan boats. I will show you what a nice place the city can be."

Megan smiled. "I would like that," she said. It had been a long time since anything had pleased her so much. She and Mike would have fun together—just the two of them! It would be almost like old times.

The day seemed endless. Megan could think of nothing else but Mike, the park, and the mysterious swan boats. School finally dragged to a close. Never had the bus ride home seemed so slow.

At long last, Megan stood before the door of Rose's corner room in the big house. Breathlessly she knocked, then stepped back, waiting for the door to open.

Nothing happened. Her heart sank just a little, but she knocked again. The only answering sound was the faint echo of her own knock down the long hall. It was plain that Rose was not there.

Tears began to roll down Megan's cheeks. She felt small, and alone, and very helpless. What

could she do? Mike would be waiting. He would
be disappointed, too, if she did not come.

Then, in a flash, Megan knew what she must
do. She must go alone. It was not very far. She had
gone with Rose a number of times. She was quite
sure that she remembered the way. Mike would be
so pleased that she had found the way by herself.

She knew the way down the long hall and out the front door. Megan slid her hand along the wall, measuring the distance. She went down the front steps, counting each one.

She heard the traffic rolling steadily past the house. Megan turned in the direction she remembered. She walked carefully and listened for every sound. People hurried by, sometimes brushing her as they passed. Everyone seemed in a very great hurry. Megan was startled by the sudden bark of a dog close by. A group of children raced past. She stepped into the path of one of them.

"Watch where you're going, Stupid!" shouted a boy's voice back at her.

Megan began to tremble. Perhaps she had better go back. She was not as sure as she had been that this was the way that Rose had taken her. Then she thought of Mike. He was waiting, and he would be so proud to think that she had found the shop by herself. She walked on slowly and steadily.

The curb appeared sooner than she had expected. Before she had time to think, her foot had slipped over the edge. She lost her balance and fell hard. Her knees scraped the rough concrete.

"Watch the light!" someone shouted.

"Look out, little girl, the light is red!" someone else called out.

Confused and frightened, Megan scrambled to her feet as fast as she could. She heard the scream of brakes and the blast of many horns close by. People shouted from every direction. She could feel the breeze of cars as they whizzed by. Megan stood perfectly still, frozen with fear, not knowing which way to turn.

Suddenly a shrill whistle pierced through the terrifying jumble of sound. A strong hand grasped Megan's arm and drew her firmly back onto the sidewalk.

"There was a red light, little girl. Didn't you see it?" a man's voice asked.

Megan made no reply. Tears were streaming down her cheeks. She was shaking from head to toe.

"No, of course you didn't," the man added more kindly, answering his own question. "Where do you live?"

"I know where she lives," another voice said. "Let me take her home." It was a voice that Megan knew. There was no mistaking Rose's happy voice. Rose took her hand and together they started for home.

Safely back in Rose's quiet room, Megan sat in a
big chair while Rose bathed her scraped knees with
cool water.

"I called Mike," Rose was saying. "He will take
you to the park tomorrow instead."

Rose's hands were gentle as they bathed
Megan's bruises and bound them with long strips
of soft bandage.

"Come," she said when she had finished. "I will show you my potter's wheel. If you like, I will teach you how to make a bowl of clay."

Rose's hands guided Megan's over the strange object that was the potter's wheel. Rose was careful to name all its parts, and explained exactly how they all worked together to form the pots and bowls that she made every day.

She put a piece of wet clay into Megan's hands. She showed her how to throw it onto the center of the wheel. She showed her how to start the wheel turning, and how to shape the mound of clay.

Megan held her breath. She forgot the terrifying sounds of traffic that had been ringing in her ears. She forgot her scraped knees. She even forgot about Mike. She felt the cool, damp clay turn beneath her fingers. She imagined a shape and felt it growing under the pressure of her hands. She remembered the sea. She remembered the sand castles that she and Mike had made. She thought of the sun going down in a pink sky.

Then, for a long time, she thought of nothing else but Rose's words and her hands, as they guided and directed her own.

By the end of the afternoon Rose was very pleased. "I never knew anyone who learned so fast," she said in amazement. "There's no mistake about it. You have a natural touch."

"I want to make a bowl for Mike," Megan told Rose, "but it must be a surprise."

Rose smiled. "Every afternoon after school we can work," she said. "I will teach you everything I know. I think it may be the nicest surprise that Mike ever had."

Megan's world suddenly seemed to be filled with sunshine. All her new experiences began to seem wonderful and exciting.

"I can't believe it," said Mike, shaking his head. "Why should things suddenly change for her?"

Rose smiled, but said nothing. She kept their secret.

The teachers were delighted. "Megan is coming into her own," they all agreed. "Why she seems to be learning faster than we can teach!"

Every afternoon, without fail, Megan sat at Rose's wheel and practiced. The cool clay slipped through her hands, and little by little she learned to guide its shape.

Finally Megan and Rose agreed that one of the bowls was better than all the others, and was ready to be finished.

"I will bake it in my kiln," Rose explained. "The heat will make the clay hard. It can have a color, too, if you like."

It took Megan no time at all to decide. "It must be pink," she declared, "as pink as the sky when the sun goes down."

Mike had no idea at all why he was being invited to Rose's room. He could not help seeing Megan's excitement as she led him quickly down the long hall to the corner room of the big house.

"It's a surprise," Megan said, "a surprise that Rose and I have been working on for a long time."

44

When the bowl was placed in Mike's hands, Megan waited breathlessly, eager to hear what he would say.

For what seemed like a very long time he said nothing at all. Then he turned to Rose. "Did she really make this all by herself?" Megan could hear the surprise in his voice.

Rose nodded. "She could be very good, Mike. She seems to know. She hardly needs to be taught."

Mike laid the bowl down carefully. He gripped Megan's shoulders with his big hands. "Someday you will have your own wheel," he said, and his voice trembled a little. "Then, when you are through with school, maybe we can be partners again in a shop beside the sea."

Megan smiled happily. The important feeling was back.

"Maybe Rose can come, too," she said. "Maybe Rose can be a partner, too."

"Maybe," Mike agreed. "Maybe she could be at that!"

"I love the sea," Rose added in her happiest voice.

Megan breathed a deep sigh. The room felt as warm as a friendly hand.

Frances Wosmek was a greedy child. In her early years she belonged to a children's newspaper club in Minnesota. Each week they awarded one entire tax-free dollar for the best poem, the best story, and the best drawing. By dividing her energies she discovered that she could manage a fairly regular income. The habit has never left her. She still divides her time among the three. Besides writing books and poetry, she designs children's products—particularly toys and fabrics. Children delight Mrs. Wosmek. That she may never forget the secret of transforming awareness to wonder, she sticks close to them. She has taught them and has raised two of them. She lives beside the ocean north of Boston with two dachshunds and a steady stream of local college students. The ocean is her inspiration. She swims in it, walks beside it, and dreams over it during all the seasons of the year.

MORRIS AUTOMATED INFORMATION NETWORK

0 1038 0033754 7

W9-BGD-523

Princess Diana

Mary Virginia Fox

ENSLOW PUBLISHERS
Bloy Street and Ramsey Avenue
Box 777
Hillside, New Jersey 07205

Copyright © 1986 by Mary Virginia Fox

All rights reserved.

No part of this book may be reproduced by any means without the written permission of the publisher.

Library of Congress Cataloging in Publication Data

Fox, Mary Virginia.
    Princess Diana.

    Includes index.
    Summary: The life of Diana, Princess of Wales, from her early upbringing to her marriage to Prince Charles and subsequent motherhood.
    1. Diana, Princess of Wales, 1961-   —Juvenile literature.
2. Great   Britain —Princes   and   princesses –Biography – Juvenile literature. [1. Diana, Princess of Wales, 1961-
2. Princesses] I. Title.
DA591.A45D5314 1986 941.085'092'4 [B] [92] 86-4451
ISBN 0-89490-129-X

Printed in the United States of America

10 9 8 7 6 5 4 3

Illustration Credits
Camera Press, pp. 17, 21, 31, 38, 44, 48, 57, 64, 72, 83, 95, 103, 106, 111, 116, 119, 123, front cover; Central Office of Information, London, pp. 12, 78, 89, 101; Mary Anne Fackelman –The White House, pp. 125.

Contents

The Royal Family

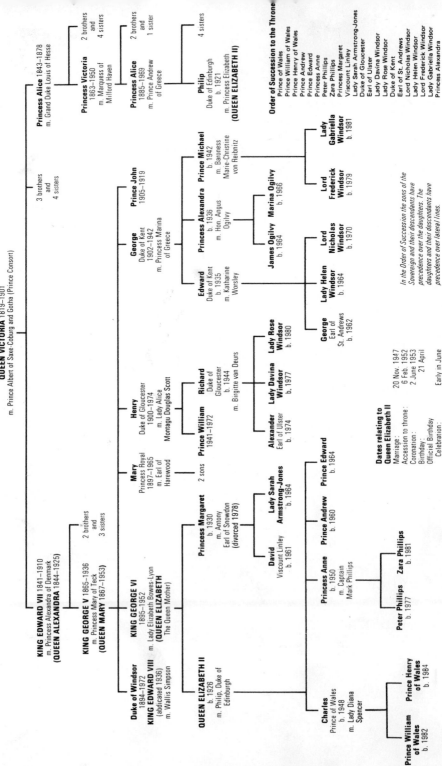

1

It happened on February 5, 1981. His Royal Highness the Prince of Wales asked Lady Diana Frances Spencer to be his wife.

The table was set for two in the prince's apartment at Buckingham Palace. A servant had brought the food but had left discreetly, closing the doors behind him. Charles was as alone as the future king of England could ever be. He had considered the question he was about to ask for several weeks. He was not at all sure that the teenager sitting in front of him, so radiant, so fun-loving, so full of life, would want to take on the weighty responsibilities of being his wife.

If their lives together did not work out as he hoped, there'd be no chance of divorce. Other members of the royal family had been granted such a dispensation, but never a future king, a person who would one day be head of the Church of England. He'd thought about all this, but had Diana?

When he asked, "Will you, could you be my wife?" there wasn't a doubt in her mind. Her smile and her eyes told him.

Still he felt he must warn her of what was to come. Their lives would always be lived in the glare of constant publicity. There would be no privacy. Their every word and gesture would be recorded; often, false meanings would be inferred from innocent remarks. He had been born with these restrictions on his life. From childhood he had been taught how to handle himself during public appearances. There was no relaxing. She'd be walking a tightrope for the rest of her life. Did she want to give up her freedom?

Diana did not hesitate. She was young, idealistic, and in love for the first time in her life. Charles was kind and reassuring. Some of their interests were different, but they had fun together. They both loved children. What better basis for a marriage?

She'd already had a taste of living in the spotlight. For the past five months, ever since she'd begun dating Charles, she'd been hounded by the press. Every time she walked out the door of her London apartment she had had to field a battery of questions while flashbulbs went off in her face. She had been amazingly patient, yet she had firmly refused to offer clues to her future plans.

The world had been playing a guessing game—"Who will Charles marry?"—since the prince was a baby. On his fourth birthday one anxious magazine editor had published a list of likely ladies he might one day marry. He'd kept them checking such lists ever since.

Rumors had been flying that "Shy Lady Di" was Prince Charles's favorite, but the press had been wrong in the past. Charles had escorted many lovely young women to social functions and had introduced them to his mother, the queen, for her approval. Various newspapers around the world had reported him engaged to at least a dozen eligible hopefuls. Now that he was thirty-one, reporters were wary of following another false clue. Nothing was certain until Queen Elizabeth herself issued the royal proclamation. In the meantime, however, speculation sold newspapers.

Diana's answer had been yes, but Charles insisted that she take time to consider her decision, "to think if it was all going to be too awful," he had said. They decided that three weeks apart would give them both a good opportunity to contemplate their futures.

She agreed, but there wasn't a doubt in her mind that if she had Charles at her side she'd be able to put up with the millions of hands to shake; the ceremonies, some bound to be boring; and the strict no-relaxing routine Charles had described to her. In fact, she was afraid that he might change his mind, but somehow the sincerity in his voice, the concern for her well-being eased her doubts.

She had been planning a trip with her mother and stepfather, Frances and Peter Shand Kydd, for some weeks. They owned a sheep ranch in Australia where they frequently spent holidays. This seemed just the right time to get away from the spotlight to a place where no one would find her. It might very well be the last time she'd enjoy the privilege.

Great care was taken to avoid notice. Mother, stepfather, and Diana were driven in a friend's car to Heathrow Airport. Today she was just another young woman wearing a head scarf, jacket, and jeans. She hadn't even needed to hide behind the sunglasses she'd stuffed in her purse.

After landing in Sydney, the three of them drove to the isolated ranch. The property bordered the vast holdings of Rupert Murdoch, one of the most powerful newsmen in the world, who owned papers in America and England as well as Australia. Any one of his reporters would have been thrilled to report the answer to the question "Where is Lady Di now?"

The British press had lost her. They were still scouting Scotland and northern England. When they finally thought to check on the whereabouts of Mrs. Frances Shand Kydd, they called her on the phone in the middle of the night. Was Lady Diana in Australia?

Frances denied it. She later admitted that this was the first and last time she had ever lied to the press. "But I was determined to have what my daughter and I both knew to be our last holiday together."

The ruse worked for a while. They enjoyed total quiet at a friend's beach house on the coast. Diana swam and surfed and caught up on some much-needed sleep, but it was not to last.

The Australian press wasn't fooled for long. The reporters arrived by helicopter and surrounded the place. Suddenly photographers were everywhere. If it hadn't been for some sympathetic friends, the vacation would have been ruined. They all banded together and kept the reporters guessing, spreading false clues and hiding Diana away first in one spot and then in another. Her stepfather made an exciting game of it. He thoroughly enjoyed speeding across the countryside losing their "tail," sending out decoys, and exchanging license plates.

The shield worked so well that even Charles had trouble getting through on the phone. He later described what happened. "I rang up on one occasion and asked to speak to her. 'No, we're not taking any calls,' was the answer. 'But this is the Prince of Wales speaking.' The reply came back, 'But how do I know it's the Prince of Wales?' 'You don't, but I am.'"

By that time he was thoroughly frustrated. Charles was not used to being put off. He was about to dispatch a member of the diplomatic corps to break the deadlock when somebody took pity on him and called Diana to the phone.

No one knows what was said, but Diana decided to return to London ahead of schedule. Again she traveled under an assumed name, and the press, expecting her to be with her mother and stepfather, was foiled again.

When she arrived in London she was given a message that Prince Charles was at his home at Highgrove busy working with his horse Allibar, which he planned to race in the Cavalry Hunters Chase at Chepstow. Diana drove from London to join him.

On the day before the race they met for lunch. Charles had given the horse a brisk workout and was quietly walking him back to the stable when suddenly the eleven-year-old horse stumbled and collapsed on the ground. Charles jumped free, realizing something was seriously wrong. He cradled the horse's head in his arms, not leaving until a vet arrived. By then the animal was dead, having collapsed from a heart attack. Charles was visibly shaken. Diana was in tears, but still the couple was obliged to leave in convoy to avoid the press. Prince Charles's car was followed by the one used by Diana, which in turn was followed by a police escort. The prince had a public appearance to make and a speech to give.

Sharing a moment of sadness seemed to bring Charles and Diana even closer together. That evening they were alone—

as alone as Prince Charles could be—comparing their thoughts and confirming their feelings for each other in words only they will ever know.

Two more official bits of business had to be taken care of before an announcement of their engagement was made. Both were mere formalities, but protocol was not to be ignored. The next day Charles phoned Diana's father in London and asked for her hand in marriage.

"May I marry your daughter?" he said simply. "I have asked her and very surprisingly she has said yes."

Earl Spencer, of course, was delighted and jokingly said later, "I don't know what he would have done if I'd turned him down."

Charles also needed his mother's official approval under the Royal Marriage Act of 1772 introduced during the reign of George III. It was granted gladly. The queen had liked Diana from the start—and it was well known that she was not always easy to please—but Charles's choice was momentously important to everyone in the country. He was not only selecting a wife, he was choosing the next queen of England.

Diana passed all the tests. If ancestry were taken into account, she could name even more relatives of royal blood than Charles. They are in fact distantly related. Both are descendants of Henry VII and James I. Her family has been close to the royal family for generations, serving them in honored positions.

Most important of all, her own reputation was spotless. It would have been embarrassing to have some former boyfriend show up in later life and sell a lurid story to a publisher, besmirching the character of the queen. When Diana had gone out in the evenings to plays or restaurants, she had frequently been escorted by young men her age, but she had never had a steady boyfriend. Her social life revolved around her school friends and roommates. They usually attended functions in groups.

Diana seemed to be the perfect choice. She appeared to be having a good effect on Charles, according to the press. The prince was thirty-one years old, an age when he should be settling down.

That Saturday night the queen held a family dinner party at Windsor to celebrate the news privately. The next day Charles gave Diana her ring. It was a large oval sapphire surrounded by fourteen diamonds, which Diana had helped select herself. It was elegant and costly but conservative in design.

On Monday the prime minister, Margaret Thatcher, and the leader of the Opposition party, Michael Foot, were told the news. Coded telegrams were sent to other heads of state. The Spencer family now sent out announcements in strictest confidence to immediate members of the family and god-parents, but it was hardly a secret to anyone close to Diana.

Her sister Sarah said afterward, "I guessed when I saw her face. She was totally radiant, bouncing, bubbling."

Knowing that it would be very hard for Diana to manage the crush of the press once the word was out, she was invited to stay at Clarence House, the residence of the Queen Mother, Charles's grandmother. On February 23, Lady Diana Frances Spencer packed her suitcase and left her roommates behind. It was the end of her life as a private citizen.

Charles wanted very much to have the official word given by the palace before anything appeared in print in the newspapers. It was not to be. Somebody had leaked the news.

Lady Diana and Prince Charles take a stroll shortly after announcing their engagement.

On Tuesday morning, February 24, the front page of the *Times* carried the headline: "Engagement of the Prince to Be Announced Today."

For once the press was right. At eleven A.M. the queen's press secretary, Michael Shea, issued the announcement. At that moment the queen was presiding over a ceremony at Buckingham Palace. The lord chamberlain stepped forward and addressed the 150 people present.

"It is with the greatest pleasure that the queen and the Duke of Edinburgh announce the betrothal of their beloved son, the Prince of Wales, to the Lady Diana Spencer, daughter of the Earl Spencer and the Honorable Mrs. Shand Kydd."

Now everyone, not just British subjects, wanted to hear about the fairy-tale princess. To help satisfy the curiosity of the press, two journalists were invited to present questions to Charles and Diana. The interview would later be shared with the rest of the reporters.

To put the couple at ease, particularly Diana, who had never gone through such an experience before, the press conference was to be held in Charles's private sitting room in Buckingham Palace, where he had proposed to her just three weeks before.

The first questions concerned the date of the wedding and their plans for the honeymoon. Then more personal questions were asked. How and when had they first met?

2

Actually neither one of them remembers the first time they met, perhaps because Diana was a pudgy baby and Charles a teenager about to go off to the Gordonstoun School. Yet it would have been surprising if their paths hadn't crossed. Diana was born at Park House, near the east coast of England in Norfolk, on Sandringham land, one of the two country estates owned by the queen, where the royal family spend both winter and summer holidays.

Although the property is actually rented from the royal family, the lease was first drawn up when King George V offered Diana's maternal grandparents the use of the house. Diana's mother was born there in 1936, and the land was later turned over to her after her marriage to Earl Spencer. It wasn't until the death of Diana's grandfather, Lord Spencer, that her father inherited the title and Althorp became the Spencer family seat. But until then the Spencers made their home in the far from modest surroundings of Park House.

It is a large house with ten bedrooms and ample servants' quarters and garages. It was built in the nineteenth century by

Edward VII when he was Prince of Wales. The house is brick and stone, rather forbidding in appearance from the outside, but it was brightened with country chintz and children during Diana's days. It is situated on a grand sweep of lawn approached by a long gravel driveway.

Diana was born on July 1, 1961. She weighed in at a healthy seven pounds twelve ounces and was hailed by her father as "a perfect physical specimen."

No name had been chosen for the new baby, so sure were her parents that it would be a boy. Already the Spencers had two daughters: Sarah, then six, and Jane, four. Their third child, a boy, had been born eighteen months previously but had died within hours after birth. Everyone had been hoping for a male heir to carry on the family name.

However, they finally settled on Diana Frances, Frances being her mother's first name. Diana was a family name dating back to the eighteenth century. The first Lady Diana Spencer was called "Di." Her grandmother had plans to make her the wife of Frederick, the Prince of Wales, but it was not until the twentieth century that a Lady Di would become Princess of Wales.

On August 30, 1961, the names were made official at the christening, which took place at the church of St. Mary Magdalene, known simply as the Sandringham Church.

Diana was the only one of the Spencer children who did not have a royal godparent, although each of the six appointed guardians had impressive credentials. John Floyd was chairman of Christie's, a prestigious firm, auctioneers of the finest works of art. There was a member of Parliament and a lady-in-waiting to the queen, but no crowned heads.

The Spencer children lived in the nursery wing, which at Diana's birth was managed by a young woman named Judith.

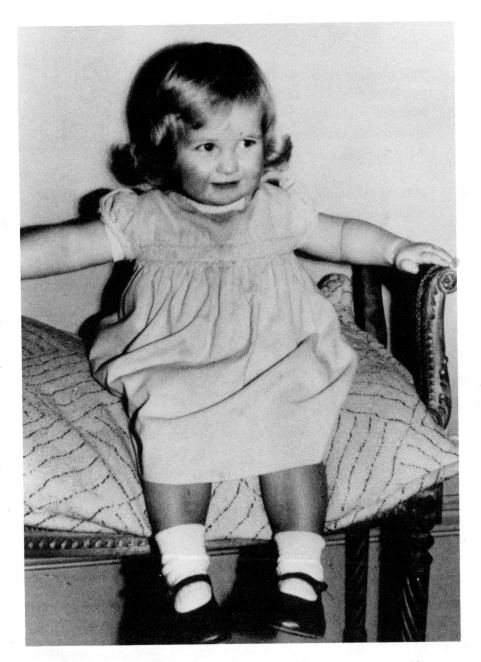

This picture from the family album shows Diana as a two-year-old at Park House.

This world of their own included three bedrooms, a bath, and one large playroom all on the second floor, set off at an angle from the main body of the house. Diana received plenty of attention as her sisters spent their mornings downstairs with the governess, who taught them their lessons.

In most parts of England in the 1960s the children would have been attending school in town, but not in this part of England, where traditions have held firm. Their governess, Gertrude Allen, affectionately known as Ally, had taught the children's mother a generation before. Most of the property in the area is owned by wealthy landowners who hire "the locals" to run their homes and their extensive farms. It has been this way for generations, and only recently have high taxes brought about any change, with some of the larger estates being sold.

Until Johnnie Spencer, as he was known to his family, inherited his own family's estate to manage, he needed something to keep himself busy. Farming was what he loved. More land was purchased around Sandringham to add to the family holdings. He continued to raise pheasants to replenish the wild game on the grounds. He was one of the best shots in the country and often hosted hunts on his property. The pastures were also stocked with fine beef cattle.

The most important addition of all was a heated swimming pool for his own family. It was frequently used by the younger members of the royal family, Prince Andrew and Prince Edward, when they were in residence in the neighborhood.

The family's fortune had always come from land. Back in the 1600s the first Lord Spencer had amassed great wealth from sheep farming. It was said that he owned at least twenty thousand sheep and had more ready money—cash, which was a rare commodity—than any other man in England. The Spencers today can hardly claim such a record, but worries over finances are rare.

Diana's own upbringing prepared her well for the life ahead of her. She was born to a family who have worked for or have been friends with the royal family for generations. Her father gave up his job as equerry to the queen when he married Diana's mother in 1954. An equerry attends all formal occasions as an aide to the queen and is present to see that ceremonies are conducted properly, to make sure that protocol is followed, and to carry out official errands for the royal family. Both Diana's grandmothers have served as ladies-in-waiting to the Queen Mother, a similar job with an honorary title.

Diana herself has been around royalty so often that she isn't overwhelmed by their presence. She knows the strict rules of etiquette that have to be followed at all times. This knowledge has been very helpful to her. When she was asked some time before her engagement whether being in the company of royalty made her feel nervous, her prompt reply was, "No, of course not. Why should it?"

But because Diana is a member of the aristocracy and not a member of the royal family, she has had a much more normal childhood than Charles. It's true she has been surrounded by servants most of her life, but when she was older she was able to go to a movie or out to a restaurant without being trailed by a royal bodyguard and besieged by the public. As a teenager she shopped for her own groceries and rode a bicycle through London traffic.

She's had a glimpse of how ordinary people live. Although as a member of the wealthy aristocracy she is unfamiliar with some of their problems, she is more understanding of another way of life than members of royalty, who are even more isolated.

She knows how to talk to people and is more at ease with the average British subject who now clamors for her attention. Charles may try just as hard to open up with people, but a certain amount of spontaneity has been polished out of him by his meticulous royal upbringing.

"Fun to be with," "thoughtful of others," "trying to please," "tidy"; these are all descriptions of Diana as a young woman. "Fresh," "sparky," and "stylish" were other words used of her, even as a youngster.

In May 1964, when Diana was almost three, her little brother Charles was born. At last there was a male heir. Flags flew that day both at Althorp and at Park House. Charles was christened in Westminster Abbey. The queen was one of his godmothers.

It was an elegant, very formal affair, and Diana had been counting on watching to see what would happen to her baby brother. She wasn't sure what the fuss was all about, but she kept asking questions and received puzzling answers.

When the great day came, she was in bed with a very sore head. She had fallen down a full flight of stone stairs. A doctor was summoned. Although she seemed to have suffered nothing more serious than a colorful bruise on her forehead, her parents decided that the trip to London would be too strenuous for her.

Diana shed a few tears and even threw a short tantrum, but she was promised a trip to London very shortly to attend her Uncle Edmund's wedding. Her mother's younger brother, the fifth Lord Fermoy, was to be married at the Guards' Chapel at Wellington Barracks.

Six-year-old Diana playing with her three-year-old brother, Charles Edward Maurice, at Park House.

Tears dried, head mended, she had her day in the great city. Even with the competition of fancy uniforms and elegant gowns, it was a picture of little Diana, perhaps a portent of things to come, that made the pages of the paper. She was wearing a fashionable coat and a jaunty hat with an upturned brim.

Now that there was someone else for Nanny to care for, Diana was promoted to the downstairs classroom for a regular schedule of classes. The schoolroom was on the ground floor between the drawing room and the kitchen. There were individual desks for each of the students. Ally, the governess, had white hair, appropriately for her sixty years, and a world of experience from teaching a handful of wealthy young aristocrats in the Norfolk area.

Diana's classes were an equal mix of listening and working. Working for her frequently meant a frantic morning of pasting and coloring and cutting, but she liked the stories and lessons she heard the older children recite. History was her favorite subject even as a preschooler.

When school was over there was usually time with Mother and sometimes Father. They might go shopping in the nearby village of Snettisham or farther to the larger town of King's Lynn. Or they might go down to the barns to see the animals. Sarah and Jane had a pony called Romany, but Diana was never very enthusiastic about being perched up on top of the frisky pet. He had a bad habit of nipping at anything in sight. Later when she was a little older she had her own pony, but one day she fell and broke her arm. After that, little furry animals seemed much more fun. She had a ginger-colored cat named Marmalade.

All three of the girls owned bicycles, but Diana, being so much younger, could not pedal quite as fast, and her nanny was not about to mount up and keep pace. During her growing-up years Diana was much closer to her brother. Sarah and Jane had their own friends and were years ahead of Diana in games and sports.

Yet she certainly couldn't be considered a lonely little girl left out of things. Special events were planned just for her. The best days of all were in summer when the family would pack a picnic lunch and drive twenty miles away to the seaside at Brancaster. They had a beach cottage there where they could change for swimming and store beach chairs, toys, and floating mats.

Sometimes neighbors were invited to come too. The Reverend Patrick Ashton and his family lived in the rectory close by. Penelope Ashton was just Diana's age. The Loyds lived across the park. Julian Loyd was the land agent at Sandringham. His children, Alexandra and Charles, were frequent playmates.

Everyone looked forward to Guy Fawkes Day, November 5, when they gathered to watch a barrage of fireworks set off by Johnnie himself. Guy Fawkes is remembered not as a hero but as a traitor who plotted to kill James I in 1605 by blowing up the Houses of Parliament. He was caught in time, but he gave the British something to celebrate with plenty of noisy fireworks ever since. At Park House hot sausages and plenty of spiced buns and punch for everybody were part of the party.

The more elegant grounds at Althorp, owned by Diana's other grandparents, were a place to be visited on special occasions, but rarely with her father. There were strained feelings between Earl Spencer and his son Johnnie. He had never quite approved of the marriage of Johnnie and Frances, and Frances had found it very hard to show any fondness in return. Earl Spencer was a man to be obeyed. He rarely took anyone's advice. People said his wife Cynthia, the countess, must have great patience to put up with his hot temper.

Yet Diana's mother dutifully took the children for visits. The four-hundred-year-old house has been remodeled several times. The original inner courtyard was enclosed, the moat filled in, and the formal gardens planted. It's been said that more royal visitors have been entertained here over the years than at any other private home in England.

The grand salon on the second floor is approached by a wide staircase that leads to a picture gallery. Park House is big by most people's standards, but it has the look of a lived-in home. By comparison, Althorp is enormous; its huge rooms have high molded ceilings, chandeliers, and marble floors and are furnished with antique furniture, priceless paintings, tapestries, porcelain, and sculpture. It was a museum, yet one member of the family remembers Diana sliding down the stairs on a tea tray. It was her first and last such adventure.

It was easier for Countess Spencer to visit Johnnie and her grandchildren than for them to make the trip to Althorp. During her frequent visits it was certain there would be special parties which the children were allowed to attend.

Life was full of exciting surprises, but at age six, Diana was not at all aware that changes were suddenly about to take place.

In September 1967 the family began to break up. First it was announced that Sarah and Jane would be going off to boarding school at West Heath in Kent. Then Frances called the children together to explain that she would be leaving too.

She had been unhappy for some time living in the country away from friends. She had fallen in love with another man, Peter Shand Kydd. He was married and had a family of his own, so no final decision about their future could be made.

A trial separation was planned. Frances would be moving to London where there was more excitement. She missed going to the theater and entertaining friends. Johnnie's chief interests were farming and shooting pheasants and woodcocks.

There were other quarrels, of course, but it was mainly a difference of disposition. Sympathy went to Johnnie, but although he was described as a "good chap" by neighbors who saw him infrequently, he tended to take after his father, who had made life at Althorp a battleground.

Frances was an independent woman and, at age thirty-one, a young woman with a life ahead of her. She did not feel she was giving up her children. Their routine was already molded by nursemaids and school. Rather than continue the bickering and unpleasantness between her and her husband, she decided the move would be best for everyone. Diana and her brother Charles were to come with her. She'd see the two older girls during their vacations. Both parents promised they'd share holidays.

Johnnie tried to talk his wife into staying. Her decision had come as a complete surprise to him, although some of their friends and particularly the household staff had been aware of the rift.

It was a confusing and unsettling time for Diana, but with the resilience of youth, she decided not to brood on what she could not change. Life in the city might be fun.

The day after Frances left, Johnnie put Diana and Charles on the train to London with their nanny. An agreement was reached that Christmas would be celebrated back at Park House.

Christmas was not a happy celebration that year. It was obvious that Frances and Johnnie were still not getting along. Both grandmothers tried to make up for the children's impending loss of their mother. Frances's mother was so shocked at her daughter's behavior that she refused to even speak to Frances, which only aggravated the situation.

Now it was a question of whether the children would stay in Norfolk or return to the city. The country life seemed more sensible for children aged six and three. They obviously adored their father. Knowing that they were being efficiently looked after by a staff of servants, Frances reluctantly agreed to let them stay for the time being. It wasn't until the next year that the courts made their residence official. Johnnie and Frances were divorced, the children's custody being awarded to their father.

Other changes were to upset their routine. Ally, the governess, left the household, and so did the familiar nanny. Another nursemaid was hired, and everyone tried to ignore the differences and put things back on an even keel. They almost succeeded.

Diana took great pleasure in giving the new nursemaid, Sally, a complete rundown on the schedule for the day. She showed her where things were kept and instructed her on how many spoonfuls of sugar she and Charles were allowed to have in their tea. Diana was the ruler of the nursery but a competent and caring child, everyone agreed. She took over the mothering of her young brother.

The staff gave her the nickname "Duchess," not because of any arrogance in her nature but because she seemed so composed for her years. She rarely cried over any disappointment. Instead she'd busy herself, almost frantically, in some form of pretend play. When she didn't exactly get her way you could tell she was angry, one friend of the family said, by the way she'd dump everything out of her drawers and then neatly arrange the contents.

She was an extremely neat little girl, even at a very young age. Her closets were always in order, and at the end of the day she never had to be reminded to put away her toys.

The Spencer children may not have been exposed to difficult academic subjects, but manners were stressed and all the traditional rules practiced: Never interrupt. Never speak with mouths full. Sit up straight at the table. Shake hands when introduced. Play quietly and be polite to visitors. Always be neat and tidy. These were lessons Diana learned well.

No one knew just how much she missed her mother. It was almost as if she refused to admit that Mummy wasn't there. When she drew a picture it was usually signed to Mummy and Daddy. She was on the go all day long, chattering constantly, but often Sally was the only one who heard the chatter. Johnnie decided in January 1968 it would be best for Diana and Charles to attend a day school in the nearby town of King's Lynn.

Diana's godmother Carol Fox suggested the Silfield School. Her two children were there, and Alexandra Loyd, Diana's friend from across the park, was also starting the same term. These familiar faces helped soften the big change of being with a group of strangers.

Diana had never been around a gaggle of boisterous children who were apt to tease and argue and fail to conform to the strict rules she was used to. Fortunately, it was a small school, with only fifteen boys and girls to a class. Understanding teachers tried hard to ease the transition.

The classrooms were housed in a row of wooden buildings in the back of a large house along Gayton Road. The house was used only for lunch break and for toilet necessities. Diana started in the first grade, Charles in the nursery section. Miss Jean Lowe, the headmistress, remembers she was pleased with the background of teaching Diana had received from Miss Ally. She had already started to read and "she had a clear good handwriting."

It was Johnnie who put on their rubbers, bundled them into scarves and jackets, and drove them to school each day.

Apparently, he was a very solicitous parent. Whenever he was out of town, which was seldom now that he was trying to be both mother and father to them, Ernie Smith, the gardener at Park House, called Smithy by Diana, took over the transportation schedule.

People were surprised that Diana had not shown more ill effects from the sudden upheaval in her life. During the first few weeks she was quieter than most, but that was probably because she had not been with groups of children before.

Charles, however, was a solemn little boy who often broke into tears. Very protective of her little brother, Diana often stopped by the nursery room at school during the day to see how he was getting along. As the weeks passed, she seemed happy and content with her new routine.

School started at nine every morning. Diana wore her uniform of gray skirt and red sweater and tights. Classes were over at three-thirty, but it was usually four o'clock by the time they were back home for tea, sandwiches, and cookies in the nursery.

In winter there was always a log blazing in the fireplace and television to watch. In summer there was the pool to enjoy. It was the only heated one in the entire area. It had a diving board and a swooping slide. There was even a revolving underwater light that flashed different colors at night.

During the week Johnnie would always come up to the nursery to spend time with Diana and Charles before they were in bed. He would hear all the news of the school day for the second, maybe the third time. He was a loving father, but there was a certain reserve he could not relax because of his own formal upbringing. Instead of warm hugs and kisses, he greeted them with a handshake. He watched them at their play without joining them. He was never on his hands and knees helping put together Charles's train.

But, to his credit, he never once discussed his feelings about his former wife with his children. Pictures of Frances were still placed on desks and mantlepieces. The children were allowed visits to be with their mother.

Diana and Charles were pleased to see her again, but it was the thought of the train trip that fired their enthusiasm for the weekend "off." Frances, in turn, tried hard not to show any emotion when it was time for their return to Park House. She felt it was easier this way without aggravating the pain of parting. But it meant that neither parent provided the warmth and closeness that many other six- and seven-year-olds experienced.

It was an atmosphere that required maturity at a very young age. School helped. There was a certain rough and tumble there to let off steam. Although Diana was one of the quieter children, she seemed to fit in well.

Miss Lowe discouraged competition. Teamwork was what counted. The school was divided into three "houses." Each student wore a distinguishing badge of red, blue, or green. If a child did well in tests, the score was chalked up to his "house." The same was true with sports. There was tennis and basketball, called net ball in England.

Diana was never considered a top student, but she always tried. Her problem was that if she didn't succeed right away, she became bored with the lesson.

"She was well behaved, but not without her moments of mischief," Miss Lowe remembers.

For her seventh birthday her father planned a special reward because she had worked so hard at school that term.

Diana at age nine enjoying a vacation at Itchenor, England.

Everything was kept a secret. A mysterious set of boxlike steps was set up in the front yard past the boxwood hedge. The twenty guests were told to line up for a game. This didn't sound like such a special treat until someone caught sight of a full-size camel ambling down the garden path. It was being led by the handler from the local zoo.

There were squeals of delight as everyone had a turn climbing aboard the swaying mount. For the first time in memory guests had to be urged to come to the table for cake and ice cream. It was a day to be remembered.

Now that the summer term was over, she went off to spend the first of many summers dividing herself between two parents. It wasn't hard to get along with Peter, her stepfather. He was so different from Johnnie. He shared his time in a different way. He didn't wait for her to lead him through the nursery to show him the stuffed menagerie she'd brought with her. Instead he taught her how to use a rowboat, how to set a lobster pot, how to fish for mackerel—things that he liked to do but that she found exciting too. He and Frances had bought a house with a big garden at Itchenor on the Sussex coast. It wasn't small, but it felt cozy, maybe just because life itself wasn't so formal under its roof. There was croquet on the lawn, not a simple little game of shooting balls through hoops but a serious test of strategy and technique that called for shrieks of glee when all went well and groans when a shot went awry.

It wasn't such a bad summer after all.

4

When she returned to Park House another change was in the planning stage. Johnnie had taken on more responsibilities. As well as managing the extensive farms he owned, he was now on the Northamptonshire County Council, was chairman of the National Association of Boys' Clubs, and was busy with various other charitable organizations. It meant that his time with the children was being cut short.

When he wasn't there, Diana's first question was always, "When will Daddy be back?" Johnnie realized what she lacked was security. He felt he knew how to provide it. She was now old enough to be able to manage boarding school.

Her aunt Lady Wake-Walker and her godmother Sarah Pratt suggested Riddlesworth Hall, near Thetford in Norfolk, where their own daughters were enrolled.

Diana very definitely did not want to leave Park House for a dormitory room. She argued strenuously. She lost. Both Johnnie and Frances had been discussing the plan for the past year. Arrangements had been made. As with other events in her life that she was unable to change, she had a way of making the best of it, of putting a wall around her emotions.

Frances tried to cheer her with a promise of a trip to Harrods, the fashionable store in London, to buy her uniforms. She'd be wearing gray divided skirts, white shirts, gray knee-length socks, and cherry red sweaters for school days. For Sundays there was a turquoise-colored light wool dress, which scratched, Diana said. In winter she'd be wearing a Harris tweed topcoat, a gray hat with a red headband, and always gloves. There was no mistaking a Riddlesworth girl. They all had the same look.

This time Diana felt overwhelmed by the change. It was a two-hour drive from Park House. How often was Daddy going to be able to make it? Would Mummy be coming too? They both promised, but Headmistress Miss Elizabeth Ridsdale, known as Riddy to the girls, frowned on family visits at the start of the term. She felt the girls had to get used to the routine without interference from the "outside."

The day she packed up and left was almost as hard on her father. He later admitted, "That was a dreadful day. . . . Dreadful losing her . . . but I knew it was best."

Diana was homesick. At first she kept to herself and didn't try to make new friends. She had the advantage of already knowing three girls who had gone to the same day school, and Alexandra Loyd enrolled the same term she did.

Riddlesworth was a small school, 120 girls between the ages of seven and thirteen. It was housed in an impressive sandstone mansion surrounded by well-cared-for grounds. The Honorable Diana Frances Spencer wasn't the only daughter of titled aristocracy. To eliminate snobbery, the school was run on democratic principles. The uniform kept any girl from showing off an expensive wardrobe. Gifts from home, even on birthdays, were prohibited, and treats of candy were rationed.

Again the school was divided into three houses, with grades tallied for the house, not given to the individual. There was competition among these groups in sports as well as grade points. The only time a girl was publicly judged on her own merits was when she took a final test before entering schools that taught the higher grades. The theory was that the teachers could tell which students were falling behind, and, with such small classes, individual tutoring could bring them back to the required level.

The day was punctuated with bells, actually a cowbell rung by one of the teachers, to send the students from one place to another. Wake-up call was at seven-thirty in the morning. Twelve girls in a dormitory room were certain to bring about confusion without a set of rules to follow.

The girls dressed themselves, then stood in line to have their hair braided. Diana hated the rubber bands. Breakfast came next. After that they returned to their rooms to make their beds, then went down to the common room for prayers and lessons. In the middle of the morning there was a short recess for milk and cookies and a visit to the Pet Corner.

Every student was encouraged to bring a pet from home. It was supposed to help with the homesickness, teach responsibility in developing "self-discipline," and incidentally help teach the facts of reproduction. Diana brought her tan and white guinea pig, Peanuts. She had won a first-prize ribbon with him in the Fur and Feather section of the Sandringham Fair the summer before. She cleaned his cage daily and was very critical of others who were lax in doing their own chores. "Bossy" was the word some of them used.

Hard courses—math, grammar, French, history, and science—were interspersed with craft and art periods. In the afternoon there was a forty-minute quiet time for bed rest and silent reading, a description that was often far from the truth.

Popular sports were field hockey and basketball in the winter, swimming and tennis in summer. Diana's favorite sport was swimming, and she was good enough to make the school team. Her other interest was dancing. She loved ballet, practicing extra hours, holding on to the back of a chair to do her stretching and practice her positions. Extra hours in the dance studio meant she missed the riding lessons offered at the same time, something that didn't bother her at all. Since falling off her pony when she was seven and breaking her arm she was not about to tempt a four-legged creature again.

There were a few lessons on Saturday as well as church practice, singing hymns that would be called for on Sunday. The high point of the week for Diana was the reward of candy on Saturdays and Sundays. Each girl had a tuck box, a small tin lock box she brought from home that was kept in the tuck room. Alfred Betts, her father's butler, remembers "a quiet, reserved girl, trying to hide the anxiety of going back to school at the end of every holiday by getting her tuck box filled up with chocolate cake, Twiglets, and ginger biscuits."

Treats were counted out carefully by the matron unless discipline for a transgression meant, horror of horrors, being denied the treat. There were a few times Diana missed her candy. She had a knack of saying things to make her friends giggle at the most solemn moments in chapel.

After her initial period of homesickness and misery, she seemed to recover her normal cheerful disposition. She was always busily involved in school activities. She was a person who wanted to be liked, to be assured that she belonged, which was complicated by the fact that where she belonged seemed to be in many places at once. Although she was not considered a leader, she was fun to be around because of her sense of humor.

Even at this age she was showing a paradoxical combination of assurance and shyness; reserved at times, the next minute she would bubble over with enthusiasm. Without being aggressive, she knew how to get her own way about most things. She was now acquiring a degree of self-confidence, beginning to display an extrovert side of her character. She loved charades and dressing up, which hinted at the dramatic flair she would later develop.

Diana's mother and father took turns coming to visit her, although they never came together. Outwardly she showed no signs of resentment that they had sent her away from home. In England especially, boarding school is a privilege children of wealthy families expect. Both of her parents were obviously concerned about her well-being. They loved her, but their caring was doled out by the hour on visiting days, not by the day or the week.

Johnnie came most often, sometimes bringing a basket of fruit for all the girls. He even braved an epidemic of mumps, against his doctor's orders, to visit his daughter who was down with a swollen face.

"He was marvelous," said the headmistress, "always interested in how she was getting along and whether she was happy."

She was growing up fast, becoming a tall, leggy girl. She often said she wished she were short and slender. Ballet dancers weren't supposed to be so tall or so fond of candy.

At the end of her first year she won the Legatt Cup for helpfulness, for volunteering to take on added chores around the school. She loved tennis, but she knew she'd never be as

Even when young, Diana enjoyed dressing up for the camera.

good as her mother, who had qualified for Junior Wimbledon in 1952. In fact, her mother had been "captain of everything" while at her school, Hatfield Heath. It was a hard record to match.

During the fall of 1972 Diana's grandmother Countess Cynthia Spencer died. Diana was very upset at the news. Her grandmother had been a figure of strength who was always there when needed, moving in and out of her life but on call for emergencies. Of the four children, only Sarah attended the funeral in Northampton, but Diana was given special permission to take time off from school for the memorial service in London at the Royal Chapel in St. James Palace. The queen mother, Princess Margaret, and the duchess of Kent were among those who came to pay their respects.

Soon after the funeral Diana's mother and stepfather moved to a remote farm on the Isle of Seil off the west coast of Scotland. It meant that her mother wouldn't be coming to the school as frequently, but some of Diana's holidays would be spent on the island, which sounded like fun.

The next big change was coming soon. Diana was outgrowing Riddlesworth Hall. As a teenager she would be moving on to a higher school.

5

West Heath, a small, select school, was where her sisters had gone. To be accepted girls had to take the Common Entrance Examination, but there were no passing or failing marks. The only qualification was a student's ability to express herself well on paper. Diana, who hated all tests, was still nervous.

In the summer of 1973 she took the tests and was accepted. Diana felt a great sense of relief. This move she didn't challenge.

West Heath was a friendly school and one with a venerable tradition. It had been established in 1865. Several of its alumnae were well known, including Queen Mary when she had been Princess Mary of Teck.

Diana settled into the school's routine better than many of her classmates. It helped to have her sister Jane and her cousin Diana Wake-Walker there too. The dormitories were named after flowers, but their furnishings were sparse. For one term Diana slept beneath a photograph of Prince Charles, showing him in his royal attire during his investiture as the

Prince of Wales. It wasn't a pinup she'd purchased herself, but a gift to the school by Cecil King, one of the school's most generous benefactors.

Roommates were chosen by lot and were changed each term, so that theoretically everyone had a chance to know a larger selection of friends. Diana again never had one very close chum, but she seemed to fit in with the group.

As in her other school, the rising bell rang at seven-thirty. Breakfast was at eight. Bathing was put on rotation, three times a week, hair shampooing once a week. Diana, who was fastidiously neat, occasionally was caught with an illegal hair wash. The girls did their own laundry.

They were allowed two weekends off each term. Diana used to spend them with her sister Sarah, and later with Jane, when they were both living in London in their own apartments. They remember that she used to spend much of her time cleaning up for them and doing their laundry when she came for visits.

Diana loved food and periodically had to put herself on a diet to keep from ballooning into a "butterball," as she once called herself. For this she seemed to have plenty of self-discipline.

Collecting mail was always a high spot of the daily routine. Both her mother and her father wrote regularly. Diana was not always prompt in answering, although the house monitor made sure some "required letters" were sent home. She never got letters from boyfriends simply because she didn't have any. There was very little opportunity to acquire them at a girls' school.

The *Daily Telegraph* newspaper was delivered every day. Her favorite sections were the fashion pages and the news of royalty, many of whom she personally knew, reported in the Court Circular. She never smoked or tried drinking gin, as some of the girls did for a lark. She was considered quite a conservative by her contemporaries. Her only temptation was candy.

Classes were unusually small, no more than eight to a section. Each girl was assigned her class according to her ability, not her age, so that it was quite possible to be ahead of one's year in some subjects and behind in others.

Diana was not much good at math, and in French she was even worse. But she'd never really traveled abroad to practice her languages, as had many of the other girls who'd spent time in Europe. Her holidays were spent with either her mother or her father.

Frances's new home on the Isle of Seil was a working ranch where they raised beef cattle and show ponies. The house was a whitewashed farmhouse set on a windy hillside where it rained almost every day of the year. Jeans were the preferred uniform. Diana came to love the place. It was the first real home she had had without the fuss and bother of strict routine. She even made friends with some of the local families. It was a part of her life, probably the only part, where she could be entirely herself. Yet she still considered Park House her real home.

There was no doubt that she looked forward to these breaks. She felt affection for her mother, although not the close attachment she might have had if their visits had been more frequent and longer.

The summer term at school, which didn't end until the middle of July, was her favorite. It was then that she excelled in sports. She won the Junior Swimming Cup and in her last

Diana and Souffle, a Shetland pony, at her mother's home in Scotland during the summer of 1974.

year the Senior Diving Cup. "When she dived," remembers her headmistress, "you never heard a splash."

She loved tennis, both playing it and watching it. During the Wimbledon matches, her mother always arranged for her to have tickets for at least one day. She was on the field hockey team at one point and also played lacrosse, which they all called lax.

At West Heath she started taking piano lessons for the first time, at a surprisingly late age considering her grandmother Lady Fermoy's passion for music. As well as being a talented pianist, Lady Fermoy was the principal sponsor of concerts at the King Lynn's Music Festival, which had won national renown.

According to Miss Rudge, the principal, "For someone who started late she made phenomenal progress. Everyone wished she'd begun to play earlier."

She practiced diligently for a year but then turned her interest to dancing. Again she took extra ballet lessons and learned to tap-dance. She worked hard at it, which proved she had plenty of tenacity when she was interested in something. She won the school dancing competition at the end of the spring term.

Rules at West Heath were rigid. If anyone was caught talking after the lights were out, her punishment was working in the garden, polishing the brass, or cleaning the bathrooms. Diana did her share when necessary without complaints.

The girls were allowed to be out of uniform on weekends. Even then it was noted that she was particularly meticulous about the way she dressed. It was always simple, but even in a pair of jeans she seemed to show a flair for fashion, combining red jeans and a striking black-and-white polka-dotted shirt for her weeding chore.

She'd often slip out to the village of Sevenoaks to buy her favorite, cream eggs. It was on one of these expeditions that she went ahead without permission to have her ears pierced at a little place called Adam and Eve. Simple studs were the only pieces of jewelry allowed at school, although she was rarely without a pendant in the shape of the letter "D," which a group of her friends had chipped in to buy for her birthday.

Although she didn't have any one close chum, Diana shared many of her interests with Sarah Robeson, who planned to work with children as a teacher when she graduated. She and Sarah used to look after the children of one of the teachers in their free time. Mr. Smallwood and his Italian wife lived in a cottage on the school grounds. The two children spoke only Italian, which sometimes strained the lines of communication, but with patience, giggles, and charades they succeeded.

Sarah and Diana always tried to be first in the dining room at supper time. They would help set up the tables so that they could reserve seats close to the door. This meant they could get out quickly on weekends and grab the comfortable chairs in front of the television set. One of their favorite programs was "Charlie's Angels."

Diana was a member of the Voluntary Service Unit. Once a week she and a friend would visit an elderly lady in Sevenoaks. They were there to give her company and to help with any chores that might be required.

When she left West Heath, she was given a special award for her service. "We don't give this every year," explained the headmistress. "It's presented only to outstanding pupils. She's a girl who notices what has to be done and then does it willingly and cheerfully."

On June 9, 1975, when Diana was almost fourteen, her grandfather died at the age of eighty-three. Diana and her cousin first heard the news from the headmistress. His passing suddenly closed another chapter in her life. Now she and each of her sisters inherited the title of Lady. Young Charles became Viscount Althorp and Johnnie the eighth Earl Spencer.

When Diana came home from summer break, everything had been packed for the move. She had mixed feelings. She didn't want to be around the dismantling of all her memories. She called her friend Alexandra Loyd, and the two of them went off to the beach cottage at Brancaster until the fleet of moving vans was gone.

Althorp, the family seat of the Spencers for 475 years, was to become their residence, but would it seem like home? She had no friends there. The great house is surrounded by a fifteen-hundred-acre estate. It holds the contents of five homes once owned by the Spencer family and houses one of the finest private art collections in Britain, if not the world. Its walls are hung with works of Rubens, Van Dyck, Gainsborough, and Reynolds. But this hardly made it home.

The next spring Diana was confirmed into the Church of England on March 12, 1976. She had received her instructions in a private class given by Canon John Rahe-Hughes. Her mother, father, and sisters all attended the ceremony.

The only change this made in Diana's routine was to permit her to attend early service on Sundays and have the rest of the morning free to read the Sunday papers and Barbara Cartland novels.

Along with the move from Norfolk to the friendless splendor of Northamptonshire came an even more dramatic change. Diana's father had met Raine, countess of Dartmouth.

Diana enjoying a visit to the Isle of Uist, Western Isles, Scotland.

The two of them had been working together on a book called *What Is Our Heritage?* to be published by the Greater London Council. Johnnie was providing the photographs. Johnnie and Raine had fallen in love.

But all was not so simple. The countess had been married for twenty-six years to someone Johnnie had known well in the days when the two of them were friends at Eton. The couple had four children, two of them adult age, two at home. Again a scandal was brewing. Raine had always been in the public eye, from the time she had been proclaimed debutante of the year to her more recent activities as a forceful member of the Westminster City Council, always sounding off on controversial subjects from banning pornographic films to the deplorable condition of refuse collection.

Raine enjoyed being in the center of attention, as did her famous mother, author Barbara Cartland. The flamboyant, blond novelist was even better known than her daughter. Diana knew her books well.

"They were really awful romantic slush novels," one of Diana's friends recalled, "and we couldn't wait for another title to be released."

After divorce proceedings that were well covered in the press, Raine and Johnnie were married on July 14, 1976. None of the Spencer family knew of the wedding until she had moved into Althorp Hall and taken over as mistress of the estate.

It was a shock to everyone. Sarah and Jane were horrified. As one friend put it, "She's not a person, she's an experience. Raine has an iron hand in an iron glove, which is so beautifully wrought that people don't realize even the glove is made of iron until it hits them."

It wasn't only the house that Raine took over; she dominated Johnnie and tried to take over the children as well. All the children had their own bedrooms, but Sarah and Jane, aged twenty-one and nineteen respectively, handled the situation by staying away from Althorp and not speaking to their stepmother.

Diana is not one to bring on a confrontation when there is another way, a friendlier way, to ease tension. She accepted the situation without greeting Raine with open arms.

Diana's room was the old night nursery on the second floor filled with Barbara Cartland novels and stuffed toys. It was close to her father's suite of rooms, but rarely did she have a chance for a moment alone with him.

Other guest rooms were frequently occupied by Raine's two youngest children, whose custody had been awarded to their father but who often spent holidays at Althorp. Charlotte was fourteen and Henry only eight. In spite of what Diana may have felt about her stepmother, she was always friendly with Charlotte and Henry, knowing only too well how alone they must feel with their lives turned topsy-turvy.

Barbara Cartland was another visitor. Wearing pink ruffles, flounces, and feathers, she had her own way of ordering the staff around to please her fancy. She insisted that her diet be fortified with natural honey, vitamin products, and ginseng, an oriental herbal root.

Diana still liked to dress in jeans and do her own washing in the servants' quarters. Raine's life-style was decidedly different. She didn't care for the country at all and rarely sauntered out to enjoy the grounds. She preferred the apartment Johnnie owned in London or the one she had in Brighton on the coast. She spent her mornings in bed, where she handled much of the office work she had now taken over from Johnnie.

To give the countess credit, she was a very practical business manager and probably saved the estate from being taken over by the government for payment of huge inheritance taxes at the death of the seventh Earl Spencer. She cut the household budget to a minimum, dismissing most of the staff.

The west wing of the house was reserved for the family. The rest of the estate was put on display to the public. Anyone with the price of admission could roam the rooms of Althorp. The stable, which was built in the same design as St. Paul's Church in Covent Garden, was turned into a tearoom, souvenir shop, and wine shop. Busloads of tourists helped pay the family bills.

Yet Raine insisted on the most formal style of living. During the afternoon she wore suits and high-heeled shoes, as she felt befitted a countess. In the evening she would change to a long dinner gown. Diana was expected to conform to the required dress code as well. As a result, Diana spent most of her free weekends with her sisters in London, rather than at Althorp with her father.

Rarely did Raine have a chance to tell her side of the story. Only after Diana's engagement to Prince Charles was an interview with Jean Rook of the *Daily Express* newspaper printed. "It was bloody awful. And all right, for the first time I'm going to say my piece because I'm absolutely sick of the Wicked Stepmother lark. You're never going to make me sound like a human being, because people like to think I'm Dracula's mother, but I did have a rotten time at the start and it's just now getting better. Sarah resented me, even my place at the head of the table, and gave orders to the servants over my head. Jane didn't speak to me for two years, even if we bumped in a passageway. Diana was sweet, always did her own thing."

Doing her own thing was the only way Diana could cope.

West Heath was a school that quite frankly didn't push academic achievements. Miss Rudge herself had set forth the aims of the school: "The training in the art of living together is the most important part of school life." There was music and sports and art and riding. It was up to the individual student to reach for the harder subjects. Miss Rudge taught Latin for those who chose the subject. No one was pushed, which may be one of the reasons that after four years Diana had not passed one of her "O" exams.

These are called Ordinary General Certificate of Education exams. They are given nationwide to all British schoolchildren when they are approximately sixteen years of age. When they are passed students go on for about two more years of study until they take the "A," or Advanced level, exams, which are a prerequisite for going on to college.

In June 1977 she failed her "O" tests in English literature, English language, art, and geography. It really wasn't because she was such a "no-hoper," the term used for the really stupid. It was just that she was lazy. One of her close friends said, "We used to spend all our time reading Barbara Cartland books when we were supposed to be doing prep. We read hundreds of them. We had a craze on them. We all used to buy as many as we could in the holidays and sneak them back in, and we'd swap them around."

Some of the girls who failed the exams dropped out, but Diana decided to stay on and retake them in the fall. However, between such books, summer sports, and holidays with parents, Diana didn't spend much of her time cramming for the exams. Once again she flunked. Yet with no real purpose to her life and no place else to go, she decided to stay for the rest of the semester or until a brighter alternative presented itself.

She had no wish to return to the home of either her mother or her father. Jane was off in Italy studying art. Her sister Sarah seemed so much older now and had her own circle of friends. Sarah had started dating Prince Charles during the summer of 1977. In fact, the press had already begun to speculate on the possibility of Sarah Spencer's becoming the next royal bride.

When Sarah met the prince, she was suffering from anorexia nervosa, a disease that tempts people to diet irrationally whether they are overweight or not. She was hospitalized for six weeks, and it was said that Prince Charles helped her cure herself. People remembered this incident later in Diana's life when she began to lose weight in a great hurry after the birth of her first son. Close friends say Diana was in no way suffering from the same compulsion as her sister. The two girls are not at all alike in disposition, with Diana being the calmer, more even-tempered one in the family.

One weekend during Diana's last term at West Heath she received permission to go to Althorp for two days. A shooting party had been arranged by Earl Spencer. Sarah had invited Prince Charles to come, and he had accepted.

6

Prince Charles arrived on a Sunday afternoon in time for a gala formal dinner. The 450-year-old mansion surrounded by an 8,488-acre estate was impressive even by royal standards. The state dining room at Althorp is one of the showplaces of the house. The table was set for thirty-two guests with the prince seated next to his host. Diana was not within earshot.

It was not until the next day that her sister Sarah introduced them formally. They were standing in the middle of a plowed field by Nobottle Wood.

On recalling the day later, Diana's father remembers that "it was Diana who was occupying his attentions. Somehow she automatically ended up standing at the side of Prince Charles."

Although this may have been the beginning of a schoolgirl crush she had on him, it couldn't be said that the prince's head was turned at that exact moment. It was only later, during Diana's first interview at the time the engagement was announced, that Prince Charles tried to recollect his first impression.

"What a very jolly and amusing and attractive sixteen-year-old. I mean great fun—bouncy and full of life and everything."

And what had Diana thought of Prince Charles? She answered, "Pretty amazing."

Amazing or not, no campaign to usurp her sister's boyfriend was ever in Diana's mind. It was obvious that a decision would have to be made about her own future. Her father advised staying on at West Heath to try her exams for the third time. The teaching staff were sure that with only a miminum of effort on Diana's part she'd be able to pass and go on for her "A" tests. But her mother had a more inviting offer. She suggested that Diana go to Switzerland, to the finishing school that Sarah had attended, the Institut Alpin Videmanette at Château d'Oex near Gstaad. Diana agreed.

The headmistress Madame Yersin recalls, "When Lady Diana arrived she was a lovely girl but rather young for a sixteen-year-old." People described her as pretty, but not the beauty she blossomed into later.

Her French teacher said, "Lady Diana was broad-minded, but she was also very idealistic about what she wanted for herself. She wanted to get married and have children of her own."

She was the perfect image of an old-fashioned girl, content to be herself without the pressure of a career.

This was the first time Diana had ever been abroad—in fact, the first time she had ever been in an airplane. She arrived in the middle of the year's term among strangers. Hardest of all, the school's strict rules forbade speaking anything but French. This had never been Diana's best subject. She was miserable.

The only thing that was fun was a chance to learn to ski. It didn't help knowing that Prince Charles and Sarah were skiing just a few mountaintops away as guests of the duke and

Diana spends a winter holiday skiing, a sport she learned while attending school in Switzerland.

duchess of Gloucester. Although it was at this time that Sarah put an end to their well-publicized friendship by speaking quite bluntly to the press.

"I wouldn't marry anyone I didn't love, whether he were the dustman or the King of England. If he asked me, I would turn him down."

When these words were quoted in the press, their friendship cooled abruptly and the dating game was over. This might have cheered Diana's hope for her own chances of becoming datable material now that the field was cleared, but actually she never considered herself in the picture. Charles was just someone to admire from afar. The only plans she had now were to return to London as quickly as possible. After just six weeks she packed her bags and left the Swiss school. It was March 1978.

She first moved into a house her mother owned at 69 Cadogan Place in London to savor her independence for the first time. Frances was rarely there.

In April Diana's sister Jane was to marry Robert Fellowes, son of the queen's agent at Sandringham. At one time he had been Prince Charles's private secretary. He was now the queen's assistant secretary. Diana was to be the maid of honor.

It was an elaborate ceremony generously paid for by Frances. Yet she stepped aside and let Raine take over the front-row seat. The wedding was attended by several members of the royal family, but not by Charles, who was attending to royal business in South America at the time.

Jane and her husband immediately moved into an apartment at Kensington Palace so Robert could be close to his employer, the queen. And when it was required that he follow the queen to Balmoral Castle for her six-week summer stay, Jane accompanied him. This gave Diana a very logical excuse to see more of the royal family while visiting her sister.

But before such plans could be put into effect Diana set about finding herself a job, a reason for being in London, which she loved. Her first paying job was looking after Alexandra, the baby daughter of Major Jeremy Whitaker and his wife Philippa. Philippa's younger brothers had known the Spencer girls, and so it was a friendly arrangement between employer and employee. Diana changed diapers, did the washing, and in return was treated as one of the family.

In the summer she returned to London. The home at Cadogan Place was a large house, and a lonely one with her mother and stepfather spending most of their time on their island retreat. Diana invited a school friend from West Heath, Laura Greig, to move in to keep her company. They were later joined by Sophie Kimball, who had stayed to finish her year of school in Switzerland.

Diana's social life, thanks to her roommates and her sisters, was never empty, but on the other hand it could not be described as wildly exciting. A usual evening would be going out to dinner at an inexpensive restaurant, or maybe sitting home with a bowl of spaghetti and watching television. Most of her friends came from the same sort of wealthy aristocratic families, yet they all had jobs of sorts or were studying art, music, or gourmet cooking. Most weekends they packed their suitcases and headed for the country, where their families owned homes. There were times Diana took friends to Althorp, but instead of staying in the big house she preferred to occupy the small house on the estate reserved for Jane and Robert when they came for a visit.

She dressed in thoroughly predictable style that fitted her taste, her allowance, and her background. England's answer to the "preppy style" of America was referred to as the "Sloane Rangers." These were the girls who bought their clothes from the fashionable shops around Sloane Square close to the "Tiara Triangle," where the most expensive designer shops were located.

The uniform of the "Sloane Ranger" was a silk scarf knotted around the neck, a single strand of pearls, a navy blue velvet jacket, a pleated skirt, or sometimes culottes or knickers (invariably navy), low-heeled shoes called court shoes, and pale stockings. She loved to shop for clothes, but she still hadn't quite made her own fashion statement. In fact, she wore her roommates' clothes almost as often as her own. They all shared wardrobes. They all had their hair cut by the same hairdresser, Kevin Shanley, but none of them wore much makeup at all.

In July Diana celebrated her seventeenth birthday and enrolled in a driving school. She failed to pass her first driver's license examination but managed to come through on the second attempt. Some of her friends admit that she was not the most cautious driver on the road. It was best to fasten their seat belts before closing the door. Diana used her mother's car, a Renault 5, but for traveling through London a bicycle was her favorite mode of transportation.

She enrolled in a three-month cooking course. She was so successful that she placed her name with an agency that provided caterers for simple parties. She was very capable when preparing canapés for cocktail parties.

A more permanent position would have interfered with

some of her spur-of-the-moment plans. Another employment agency booked her for babysitting and light housecleaning, which she really didn't mind at all. It was unusual training for a future queen.

In September the Spencer girls received the frightening news that their father, aged fifty-five, had collapsed in his office at Althorp with a cerebral hemorrhage. Raine, who had been in London at the time, rushed home to take charge. Johnnie was taken first to the local hospital, Northampton General, and then to the National Hospital in Queens Square in London.

He was in a coma for several weeks. Doctors informed the family that he stood only a 50 percent chance of surviving and less than that for recovering without serious handicaps. Raine would not listen to the dire predictions. She was determined to improve his chances by taking him from hospital to hospital and from specialist to specialist. She became fiercely protective and refused to let even the family visit.

Sarah, Jane, and Diana would wait until they saw their stepmother leave the hospital and then sneak in for visits. Although Raine did make life difficult for the girls, even her enemies admit that it was her single-minded devotion and determination that brought him through the crisis.

As she said in an interview with Jean Rook of the *Daily Express*, "I'm a survivor, and people forget that at their peril. There's pure steel up my backbone. Nobody destroys me, and nobody was going to destroy Johnnie so long as I could sit by his bed and will my life force into him."

In November, just as he was beginning to improve, an abscess that had formed on his lung burst. He was moved immediately to the intensive care section of Brompton Chest Hospital. Raine used her influence to obtain for him a "miracle drug," Azkocillin, which was available at that time in Germany but not in England. Immediately his lungs began to clear, and he was finally released from the hospital in January.

However, for the first month Johnnie and Raine reserved a suite of rooms at the Dorchester Hotel so that he would be close to medical care if necessary. His recovery continued, although he did not completely regain his strength and had to give up some of his responsibilities in the county. Some say it is miraculous he pulled through without more serious disabilities. His right arm is slightly paralyzed and his speech is slurred, but Earl Spencer gives credit to his wife: "She saved my life. I love her dearly."

In January 1979 on the very weekend her father came out of the hospital, Diana and Sarah were at Sandringham as guests of the queen for a shooting party. This was really the first time Diana had been included in such an invitation. She was still quite young and not as strikingly attractive as she is now. Her shoulder-length hair was darker. She wore rather conservative clothes, and she was very shy around strangers. This lack of sophistication turned out to be a plus, however. She wasn't considered one of the pack chasing after Charles.

Charles certainly had no serious feelings toward her. It was simply refreshing to be able to be with someone who was good company and with whom he could relax. It was also flattering to be admired so obviously by Diana. From that weekend on, Prince Charles called her quite frequently, sometimes on the spur of the moment to even the number of couples in a group. Other times he would call her specifically to accompany him to the opera or ballet.

That same month she applied for a more permanent job. She loved dancing and she loved children. Betty Vacani's Dancing School was well known throughout London as the place where titled and wealthy families sent their tots to learn the finer points of rhythm and toe pointing. Even Prince Charles had suffered through the rudiments of dance with Miss Vacani.

Diana was accepted as a student teacher. She bicycled to school each morning to help with the tiny tot class. Twenty two-year-olds either suffering from acute shyness or noisily showing off were enough to test the patience of any non-experienced adult. It did not help to have the critical eyes of mothers and nannies watching her every move.

There were older classes too, with five-to-sevens and seven-to-nines. The actual routines were led by two professional instructors; Diana was simply there to help out. She enjoyed her own dancing, but she had discovered she was not cut out for this sort of teaching. After dropping this job, she went off to the French Alps for a bit of skiing.

When she turned eighteen that summer she inherited a rather large trust left by her American great-grandmother Frances Work. Instead of using it all up in some wild spending splurge, her mother suggested that she buy an apartment as an investment, preferably one large enough so that she could share it on a rental basis with friends.

Sarah, who was working with a real estate firm, found just what was needed in a four-story brick building on the corner of Old Brompton Road in the Earl Courts area, Flat No. 60 on the corner of Block H. It was in an older building with high ceilings and spacious rooms. There were three bedrooms. Sophie Kimball moved in as soon as the bare essentials had been selected. The furnishings were nothing

A serious Diana pondering her future with the Prince of Wales.

very elegant, but they were serviceably comfortable. Philippa Coaker, a friend of Sophie's, made up the trio. Diana continued to shop for the apartment but always brought back samples to show her roommates before a final decision was made on the purchase. There was a homey atmosphere to the place. The hallway was cluttered with bicycles and the living room with magazines.

In the fall she started her first really regular job at the Young England Kindergarten in St. George's Square, Pimlico. It was through her sister Jane that she got the job, her sister having known one of the young women who ran the school. They needed an assistant for an afternoon group of children three days a week.

The school was held in a large, bright church hall with a blue-curtained stage at one end. The walls were decorated with child-produced works of art, and the atmosphere was friendly. Diana had finally found her niche. She loved her work, which meant policing the noisiest offenders and tidying up after paint and paste sessions. She fit in so well she was asked to work in the mornings as well.

The school set their enrollment at fifty, and there was always a waiting list. The children, aged from two and a half to five, included offspring of successful lawyers, bankers, and politicians. Two of the enrollees included Sir Winston Churchill's great-granddaughter and the great-grandson of former Conservative Prime Minister Harold Macmillan.

This schedule still didn't fill all her day. She took on a part-time job caring for a young American boy named Patrick Robinson, whose father was an officer of an American company headquartered in London. She would play with him by the hour and then take him for long walks in his stroller, sometimes combining her own shopping with his entertainment.

At Christmas Philippa Coaker moved out of the apartment to travel abroad and Virginia Pitman, another friend of Sophie's, moved in to take her place.

Diana and her friends, a very conservative group of teenagers, didn't smoke or drink. Most of the time they went out as a group rather than on individual dates.

Virginia Pitman described what life was like. "She had a lot of friends. A few people came around for supper, that sort of thing, and she sometimes went to the ballet or the cinema and occasionally out to dinner, but she didn't go out a great deal at night. She liked to stay home and watch the telly and have a very quiet evening. . . . We often came back and found her dancing around the flat, just on her own. Her favorite pop group at that time was Abba."

She loved to dance but she disliked nightclubs, probably because the people who went there were dramatically sophisticated. It made her feel insecure. She never felt comfortable with groups outside her own friends.

Diana particularly loved the ballet. Even when she didn't have an escort, she'd ask her grandmother Lady Fermoy to arrange for tickets. At this time in Diana's life she saw much more of her grandmother than her mother, who had sold her apartment in London and now divided her time between the faraway farms in Scotland and Australia.

There were two more changes of roommates in 1980. Sophie moved out and was replaced by Carolyn Pride, a friend of Diana's from West Heath. A talented student at the Royal College of Music, she moved in with her piano. Ann Bolton, who was working in the same office as Sarah and who needed a bed-and-board space, swelled their number to four.

All the girls paid rent and shared costs and kitchen duties. They were four like-minded girls with few cares and few financial worries.

Prince Charles continued to call every few weeks, but he never came to the apartment. They would always arrange to meet at the theater or wherever they were going. Diana was just one of the many young women whom the prince was seeing, and nobody placed much importance on the name Lady Diana Spencer.

7

Prince Charles had a habit of falling hopelessly in love with whomever he was dating consistently at the moment. His current flame was Anna Wallace. She was twenty-five years old and the daughter of a Scottish landowner. She was beautiful and sophisticated, with a fiery temperament not particularly suited to a future queen of England. And besides, she admitted to having had previous lovers. Charles was more bedazzled than ever by Anna and, disregarding all advice from his family and close associates, he reportedly asked Anna to become his wife.

Anna turned him down. She had no wish to sacrifice her freedom. They continued to see each other for several months more, however. The Prince of Wales was not about to take no for an answer.

The end came in June of 1980 in a fiery confrontation. It started at the queen mother's eightieth-birthday ball at Windsor Castle. Anna felt Charles had paid too much attention to other guests. She was heard to say, "Don't ever ignore me like that again. I've never been treated so badly in my life. No one treats me like that, not even you."

On the next occasion when they were in public together, at a ball at the home of Lord Vestey, he behaved the same way. This time Anna Wallace didn't put her anger into words. Instead she borrowed Lord Vestey's car and drove herself back to London alone. This was the last of their dates together, and within a month she became engaged to and then married another man, the Honorable John Hesketh.

Prince Charles was accustomed to women treating him with the respect due the future king of England. This was a terrible blow to his pride. It took this rejection to make him contemplate what he was doing with his life. He had been playing the field long enough. He should be taking his life and his future choice of companions more seriously.

Back in 1977 he had been quoted as saying that in the choice of a wife he should be guided by his head, not his heart. He had also been quoted in an interview when he was twenty-seven that he thought thirty "about the right age for a chap like me to get married." He had passed that time in life.

Diana appeared at the right moment. She was a friend, cheerful, affectionate in a sisterly way, and nondemanding.

The number of calls to her apartment increased. In July 1980 she received two invitations, one to watch him play polo with Les Diables Bleus in Sussex and another to a ball at Goodwood House. Diana called on all her roommates for advice on what to wear. She eventually packed two gowns and waited to see what the other guests had chosen. She wore a modestly ruffled blue dress and borrowed jewelry from her grandmother to match.

A week later came another invitation, this time from Prince Philip to join the royal family on the royal yacht *Britannia* to watch the Coews Week Regatta. Prince Andrew and Prince Edward were on board. So were their cousins James and Marina Ogilvy, children of Princess Alexandra. It was a young group. Diana had fun, although she was not particularly paired off with Charles. Yet after she returned to London two dozen roses were delivered at her apartment at Coleherne Court. It was the beginning of a courtship, one they both tried to hide from the press as long as possible.

With the roses came an invitation to join a group at Balmoral. This wasn't the first time she had spent the weekend at the royal family's Scottish home, but this, according to Prince Charles, was when they both began to "realize there was something in it."

So did the press, although they weren't exactly sure who the young lady was who had been sighted on the banks of the River Dee. She had been sitting quietly half hidden by a tree. She had noticed the approach of two photographers, and so as not to attract attention she had watched them in her hand mirror. The photographers were trying to get within camera range to take a picture of the Prince of Wales fishing for salmon when they were surprised by a flash of sunlight from the mirror. As they moved in, the mysterious stranger sprinted up the hill without being identified. She was wearing a man's hat and a head scarf, a checked shirt, a chunky sweater, slim corduroys, and green boots, but she had been careful to keep her face hidden.

Who was she? One man, James Whitaker, had been pursuing Prince Charles full time as a reporter from the *Daily Star* for seven years. No secrets could be kept from him for long. He found out who had been invited for the weekend by stationing himself and his co-conspirators at every exit from the estate on a twenty-four-hour alert. Lady Diana matched

Diana spending an afternoon fishing at Balmoral.

the general physical description of Charles's companion that day. At five feet ten, she was the only one that tall. Now, with a name to follow up, all he had to do was find Diana's address.

The next morning he was on her doorstep early enough to watch her head down the street to the nearest grocery store to pick up a quart of milk for her breakfast. A flashbulb and camera recorded the errand. With monumental presence of mind, she smiled sweetly and ignored the questions that were shouted at her.

From that moment on, newspaper reporters would not leave her alone. She tried to carry on her life as if nothing unusual were happening. The only change in routine was that she gave up her bicycle and used her car in London traffic.

She was polite to the press, never turning them down with a blunt "no comment" when they besieged her with questions. Sometimes she would giggle. Sometimes she would purse her lips seriously and then burst out laughing. She succeeded in charming them all, but when asked if she were in love with Prince Charles, she blushed. "You know I can't talk about my feelings for him."

It didn't take much guessing to interpret Diana's feelings, but what about Charles? There had been too many false assumptions before. They would just have to wait and see what developed.

The only time that Diana tried to argue with the reporters was on September 18 when they followed her to the kindergarten where she worked. They were upsetting the little children, who couldn't understand why there was such a crowd of people taking over their playground, snapping pictures and generally overrunning the area. Diana agreed to pose for pictures in the small park next to the nursery if they would go away for the rest of the day and leave her alone.

The result was a series of pictures that made the front pages of every newspaper in England. The photographers had knowingly posed her standing with her back to the sun. Diana was wearing a simple printed cotton skirt, a shirt, and a sleeveless sweater. The only problem was that, because it was a hot day, she had neglected to wear a slip. In the resulting pictures, the skirt was almost transparent.

When the pictures appeared Diana was horrified. In tears, she vowed she would never again be so naive as to trust the press. What was the royal family going to say?

It's said that the prince was amused. He was overheard saying, "I knew your legs were good, but I didn't realize they were spectacular. And did you really have to show them to everybody?" The rest of the family took the incident in stride. Their support gave her confidence that she'd be able to handle the pressure.

One hint that the prince was finally thinking of settling down was that he suddenly had an interest in house hunting. Buckingham Palace issued instructions to the management of the duchy of Cornwall, which is responsible for the thousands of acres owned by the prince as his birthright, to look for a suitable country home for the next king of England.

The one Charles favored was the Highgrove estate in Gloucestershire near the tiny village of Doughton. There was a gracious Georgian home surrounded by 346 acres of farmland. With four reception rooms, nine bedrooms, six bathrooms, and a fully contained nursery wing, it seemed ideal. But before making the final purchase, Charles wanted Diana to see the property.

At first she didn't say a word. The house was in something of a mess—partially furnished, in need of interior paint, and not half as impressive as Althorp. Was this really a suitable home for a future king of England? Charles watched her closely. As she moved from room to room she nodded her head and smiled. It was light and airy, not some ugly mausoleum to be a showplace for royal trappings. She began to visualize it as it might be with the right touches. But she was not at all sure those touches were to be hers. It was the newspapers that were assuming much more than was the truth.

Charles and Diana stayed at the Ritz Hotel in London for Princess Margaret's fiftieth-birthday party. The next day Charles boarded the royal train and went off to the west of England on an official visit. That night he slept aboard the train, which had pulled into a siding in the railroad yard.

The Sunday *Mirror* ran a story suggesting that Diana had driven from London to meet the prince in secret. The headlines this time read, "Love in the Sidings."

Diana was shocked and said the story was all lies. She issued a denial, insisting she had been home in the company of her roommates. The paper called up to apologize, but as Diana said later, "The trouble is people believe what they read."

Prince Charles and the queen were equally furious. It was not so much for Charles's sake—he was used to the unprincipled tactics of some of the more lurid newspapers—it was in defense of Diana's reputation that they demanded a retraction. However, the editor refused to retract the story. He said he believed it was true and that it in no way reflected badly on Diana; it just proved that she was in love with the prince, willing to drive a hundred miles through the night just to see him for only a few hours. The correspondence between palace and editor was published, bringing even more attention to the story.

In the early days Diana had thought all the publicity quite a joke. Now she was panicky. She was afraid to leave her apartment alone even to go to the nearest candy store to satisfy her perpetual craving. The queen, who very much approved of Diana as a future daughter-in-law, was afraid that so much pressure would send her away, even if Prince Charles did propose. She was harassed constantly. At one time she was forced to flee a department store in London by dashing out the fire door and climbing over garbage cans. Yet one of the photographers captured the "escape" on film. No one, not even the queen herself, had been hounded so persistently by the press. Diana's mother, as well as the queen, begged the editors of Fleet Street (a term used for the London newspaper district) to stop. She wrote, "May I ask the editors of Fleet Street, whether, in the execution of their jobs, they consider it necessary or fair to harass my daughter daily, from dawn until way after dusk? Is it fair to ask any human being, regardless of circumstances, to be treated this way? The freedom of the press was granted by law, by public demand, for very good reasons. But when these privileges are abused, can the press command any respect, or expect to be shown any respect?"

Sixty members of Parliament framed a motion in the House of Commons "deploring the manner in which Lady Diana Spencer is treated by the media" and "calling upon those responsible to have more concern for her individual privacy."

But the public continued to want to hear more about the pretty young girl who had caught the eye of the prince, and the papers intended to satisfy that curiosity.

As the prince's thirty-second birthday approached, everybody was certain that there would be an announcement about his future. Lady Diana was smuggled into Sandringham for the party, but the day came and went without an announcement.

Soon afterward the prince left on a three-week trip to India and Nepal. Diana was left to deny the allegations on her own. Her behavior throughout had been exemplary. She had shown considerable courage in dealing with the media. She had not resorted to rudeness, and her only comment in response to questions concerning the prince had been a blush. She called the regulars she recognized by name and always greeted them with a polite good morning, although she sometimes must have felt like shouting at them to leave her alone. Her very manner of handling these confrontations was a test she passed with flying colors. She had the royal stamp of approval.

When the prince returned from India in December a meeting was arranged, not at the great Balmoral Castle, but at the Queen Mother's residence in Scotland, Birkhall. This was the first time Prince Charles's grandmother had ever served as a matchmaker, and it is quite possible that Diana's grandmother Lady Fermoy, the Queen Mother's lady-in-waiting, had also discussed the future of her favorite relative with her employer.

To get out of London without being followed took planning. Diana packed her car as if going away for the weekend, tucking in a suitcase, a topcoat, and a pair of boots.

On one occasion, the Queen Mother acted as matchmaker to Charles and Diana when she invited Diana to her home in Scotland.

Then she turned as if remembering something she wanted to buy at one of the stores around the corner. The ruse worked. She and Charles had a happy weekend together, properly chaperoned by Grandmother of course, before reporters gave up watching her car.

Diana and Charles spent Christmas apart, the prince at Windsor Castle, Diana at Althorp with her father. She was suffering through a bout of the flu. The royal family moved on to Sandringham to welcome in the new year. They were surrounded by the press trying to get a picture of Diana. Suddenly they began to understand what she had been going through. Photographers were wedged in trees and perched on garden walls, all with long-range camera lenses focused on anyone who popped up in sight.

The royal family lost its customary cool. Prince Charles appeared and offered himself for five minutes of picture taking if they would go away. His greeting was, "I should like to take this opportunity to wish you all a very happy New Year and your editors a particularly nasty one."

When they still wouldn't leave, someone fired a shotgun over the head of one photographer. They finally took the hint. Soon afterward Lady Diana drove up to Sandringham for the day. They'd missed her.

With such pressure from an army of reporters, Charles and Diana decided to cancel their skiing vacation together in the Swiss Alps. On January 23 Prince Charles flew to Zurich alone. He admitted afterward it hadn't been much fun.

Two days after he returned from Switzerland the world's most eligible bachelor finally committed himself. Over a candlelit dinner in his three-room apartment at Buckingham Palace, he proposed to Lady Diana Spencer. She would have her three weeks in Australia to think about her answer.

8

Diana's return to England had been carefully arranged to coincide with Prince Andrew's twenty-first birthday, when public attention would be focused on this royal milestone.

Charles and Diana's next meeting was at Highgrove, the day the prince's horse died. Both of them were visibly shaken by the event, but their public lives had to go on without interruption. They left in separate cars. Charles had to be in Swansea that afternoon to receive the keys to the city and smile graciously for the hundreds of people who had been waiting in the freezing cold to greet him.

It was on this day that Charles decided there was no longer any reason for keeping the news to themselves. The official proclamation was issued.

Outside the palace the band of the Coldstream Guards struck up the tune "Congratulations." In the small village of Doughton, where Highgrove, the royal couple's future home, stands, the occasion was marked by a red carpet in the one and only telephone booth.

Michael Shea, the queen's press secretary, was called back from a holiday to handle the interviews. Both Charles and Diana were nervous.

The questions concerned when Charles had proposed, when and where they would marry, and where they would live after the wedding.

Grania Forbes of the Press Association asked were they bothered by the age gap between them.

Charles said, "It's only twelve years. Lots of people have got married with that sort of age difference. I just feel you're only as old as you think you are. . . . Diana will certainly help me keep young. . . . I think I shall be exhausted!"

What sort of a Princess of Wales would Diana be? Charles answered for her, "I'm sure she'll be very good. . . . She'll be twenty soon, and I was about that age when I started. It's obviously difficult to start with, but you just have to take the plunge."

"I'll take it as it comes," said Diana. "It's always nice when there are two of you and there's someone there to help you." She added that his support had been "marvelous, oh, a tower of strength."

"Gracious," exclaimed the prince.

Lady Diana giggled, "I had to say that because you're sitting there."

It was the sort of remark a royal princess would hardly have made, but the press loved it. She was human.

She proudly showed off her engagement ring, trying to hide the fact that she bites her fingernails. Copies of the ring were about to go on sale in every jewelry store in the land.

After lunch with the queen and Prince Andrew, it was time for another ordeal before the cameras. It was the first time she had agreed to pose for a photographer since the see-through-skirt incident five months earlier. She chose to wear a conservative two-piece blue suit and this time a slip.

An informal study of Prince Charles and Lady Diana showing her sapphire and diamond engagement ring.

Next came a television interview, but most of the same questions were asked. Diana's reply to the question of what she and Charles had in common was their sense of humor and every outdoor activity, "except I don't ride. Lots of things really."

"And I suppose you're in love?" one interviewer dared question. Diana answered without a moment's hesitation, "Of course."

Charles was more guarded. "Whatever 'in love' means."

Diana moved out of Coleherne Court on Monday afternoon. It was felt she needed protection against the press, which could be provided at Clarence House, the London home of the queen mother. She left a poignant note for her roommates giving them her new phone number. "For God's sake ring me up—I'm going to need you."

Diana didn't actually stay at Clarence House for long. Instead she was given a suite of rooms at Buckingham Palace where it was felt she wouldn't be as lonely. Actually she did a lot of traveling around in the five months before her wedding. She spent some of her time with her sister Jane at Kensington Palace and some with her mother, who had rented an apartment in Warwick Square. They went shopping together.

The shy young teenager very quickly emerged as a glamorous young woman, and it wasn't just a new wardrobe that did it. Being engaged gave her security and a confidence in herself that her fragmented life had never provided before. After all, she had won out over a prodigious field of competitors to become the Princess of Wales, Countess of Chester, Duchess of Cornwall, Duchess of Rothesay, Countess of Carrick, and Baroness of Renfrew. As wife of the eldest son of the sovereign, she would be addressed as "Your Royal Highness." It would have been very unusual for any normal nineteen-year-old not to be just a little in love with the pageantry of her new life-style as well as with her future husband.

She was shy at times, but Diana had already shown a strong side to her character. She had had little mothering in her lifetime, and to make her way so often alone had taken a certain toughness. Her shyness was more a lack of confidence. There was a time when her life seemed quite pointless. She had not succeeded very well in school, and her only accomplishments so far had been her ability to handle children, clean house, and do the laundry.

Now that she had security and love, she stepped forward as a person in her own right. She couldn't help feeling the approval of the crowds who surrounded her in public. It was nice to be liked. She began to make bolder decisions. At first it was shown in her clothes.

The first public affair Diana and Charles attended after the announcement of their engagement was a charity gala at the Goldsmith's Hall in the city of London. The press, of course, was there to record the event. Diana arrived in a dramatic low-cut strapless gown of black silk, a far cry from the demure little frocks she had dared to wear before. She looked stunning, but it was indeed a different picture of the princess than the public had glimpsed before.

Diana had always shown a flair for fashion even during her conservative schoolgirl period. She'd known how to add that one individual touch that could put style into even a school uniform. But right now in her life it was helpful to have some expert advice.

Diana's sister Jane had worked as an editorial assistant in the London *Vogue* magazine offices in Hanover Square. She had friends who were still constantly in touch with the fashion world. Every month dozens of outfits sent by designers who hoped to get a showing in the magazine came through their offices. Diana was able to drop by and privately see the newest and most luxurious fashions in the world. It was a wonderful way to window-shop. If she liked what she saw, she could then make an appointment with a specific designer and save a great deal of time and effort. She also had the advice of Beatrix Miller, editor in chief of the magazine; Grace Coddington, herself once a well-known model; and Ann Harvey, one of the fashion editors.

They were very helpful in advising her what outfits might be suitable for certain occasions. Not only did she have to decide on her wedding gown and her trousseau, she needed outfits for her honeymoon in the Mediterranean and for later visits to colder Scotland and for all the appointments she would be accepting during the engagement. It was a monumental task but one that Diana loved.

Diana had been photographed that fall for *Vogue* in a pink chiffon blouse with a soft flounced collar. It was just the sort of feminine style she adored. Later she called her friends on the magazine to find out where she could buy the blouse. It had come from the studio of David and Elizabeth Emanuel.

She phoned them to make an appointment. At first they thought it was a hoax. It couldn't be the Lady Diana Spencer whose picture had been in all the papers. When they found out it was indeed the fashionable young lady, they brought out all their sketches and samples for her to see. Their romantic styles suited Diana perfectly. It was the Emanuels who designed the show-stopping black strapless gown that had caused so much comment.

When it came time to choose the designer of her wedding gown, Diana again turned to the Emanuels. It was a gigantic challenge for them, but they were delighted. The publicity was worth a fortune. Actually, Lady Diana was never even charged for their elaborate creation.

First they asked the lord chamberlain whether the dress had to have a bulletproof underlining. President Reagan had recently been shot, and everyone around the world had the jitters. The answer was no.

The Emanuels maintained absolute secrecy so that no one would know the design of the bridal gown until the day of the wedding. They employed a security firm around the clock and installed a safe so that the dress under construction could be hidden away without the slightest chance of anyone breaking into the establishment to make a copy. Still, they found their trash bins were being searched, so at the end of the day any scraps of fabric from the bridal gown were burned.

No details were overlooked. David Emanuel went to the Royal Mews to measure the glass coach that Lady Diana and her father would take to St. Paul's Cathedral. Some way had to be devised to fit the yards of dress and train into close quarters.

Others were working for perfection. Beauty editor Felicity Clark gave Diana some professional advice on her makeup. She had never worn very much, and a heavy hand would have been a mistake, but Felicity offered some hints about coloring and application that were invaluable.

About this time Diana tried hard to improve her posture. Like many tall people, she tended to hunch her shoulders and lower her head as if to minimize her height. Her future husband was only half an inch taller than Diana, but with lower heels, which she had always worn, there was no evident difference in their heights. She must keep her head up.

While Diana was in the midst of the flurry of preparations, it was still business as usual for Charles. A five-week tour had been scheduled that would take him around the world, first to New Zealand and Australia, then to Venezuela, and finally to the United States. Diana drove with Charles to the airport to say good-bye. He kissed her just before boarding the plane. She kept a smile on her face until the plane was out of sight; then she broke down in tears. The public adored her for being so much in love.

Charles phoned her every day, but the harsh reality of being in the public spotlight came to the fore again. It was reported that Charles's phone had been tapped and recordings made, which had been sold to a German magazine. Immediately legal action was taken to prevent the tapes from being published in Britain. As it turned out the story was false, but it put them on guard to protect their privacy.

It was the summer of The Wedding. A whole generation of young women and some old ones too adopted Diana's hairstyle. There were Diana look-alike contests. Her picture and that of Prince Charles was seen on every type of souvenir from ash trays to jigsaw puzzles. Stamps from over seventy countries throughout the world featured Prince Charles and Lady Diana.

One weekend when Diana was at Althorp visiting her father, she offered to drive Betty Andrew, the housekeeper, into the nearby village. Before heading back she popped into a general store to buy herself a popsicle. She was dressed in jeans and a sweater. The owner took one look, then a second,

His Royal Highness Prince Charles, Prince of Wales, in the uniform of a Commander of the Royal Navy.

and stuttered. "It's not. . . . Oh, my wife will be furious that she wasn't here to see you. She's out buying more mugs with pictures of you on them to put in the shop."

Diana giggled, "Oh God, I'm sorry."

For her own cups she chose Tosedale by Aynsley China Ltd. It was estimated that the royal couple received at least ten thousand presents. About a tenth of them were put on display at St. James Palace following the wedding. Admission was charged and a considerable sum raised for charity.

She spent days answering letters from the hundreds of friends and strangers who were wishing her well and showering the happy couple with gifts. Oliver Everett, a foreign service diplomat, was called in to work as Diana's private secretary, at least during these weeks of heavy responsibility.

Six women from the Wrens (Women's Royal Naval Service) were assigned the job of helping. Diana personally answered every one of the letters she received from the people whom she knew. They were not just brief notes, but newsy letters telling what her life was like now, how busy and excited she was. She would have gotten an "A" from the headmistress at West Heath if she'd seen her now.

There were moments when she tried to bring a bit of sanity back to her hectic life by returning to old haunts. She visited the kindergarten where she had worked. The children greeted her as if nothing very special had happened since they'd last seen her. It was a refreshing change.

She also took up dancing again. She arranged to have Wendy Vickers give her private lessons at Buckingham Palace. Two mornings a week Wendy would arrive with her pianist. Diana enjoyed both ballet and tap dancing. It was her own way to escape the tension of the moment, something she had enjoyed doing since childhood.

It was the first time the palace staff had heard the strains of "Hello Dolly!" and the Fred Astaire classic "Top Hat, White Tie, and Tails" floating down the hallowed halls.

Although Diana didn't share Charles's interest in horses, she dutifully attended polo matches and steeplechase races, which she began to dread. After losing Allibar to a heart attack, Charles was working with a new mount, Good Prospect. During a period of five days Charles took two bruising falls. No bones were broken, but it was pointed out to him by other members of the family that he'd put a crimp in more than his own plans if the wedding had to be performed in a hospital room. There'd be no way to postpone the ceremony now that heads of state were juggling their calendars to attend the affair. He obliged by cutting back on his schedule, but he did not give up all equestrian events.

Just five days before the wedding Diana was on the sidelines watching Charles play polo at Tidworth. When the crowds began to surround her, she broke down and ran off in tears. The next day the newspapers played up the event as if she were cracking under the strain and should be committed to a mental institution.

Diana was quite simply exhausted. She had lost fifteen pounds since she had first been measured for the wedding gown, which meant that extra fittings had to be worked into a calendar already crammed full of duties.

On Monday, July 27, the big day had almost arrived. That night the queen gave a dinner party at Buckingham Palace for relatives and close friends. It was one of the few times that Diana's mother and father, with their respective spouses, had been together. The dinner was followed by a huge reception and dance. The ballroom was decorated with clusters of balloons bearing a feathered insignia belonging to the Prince of Wales. The last guest did not leave until the wee small hours of the morning, but Lady Diana Spencer went to bed early.

Already thousands of people were pouring into the city, and some brave souls had set up camp along the parade route. The crowds watched the Horse Guards and the carriages rehearse the route they would take to the cathedral. It was said that fifteen thousand people visited St. Paul's that day to see for themselves where the wedding would take place.

Westminster Abbey had been traditionally the setting for royal weddings, but St. Paul's can hold several hundred more guests. Also, it is more open in design. Vision is unimpeded by the screen that in the medieval abbey separates the choir and the clergy from the congregation. At St. Paul's every moment of the wedding would be photographed for the world to see. Besides, Diana's mother and father, whose marriage had ended in disaster, had been married at Westminster Abbey. Diana was glad of the change.

On the day before the wedding the world's largest tea party was held along Oxford Street. Thousands of children were served hamburgers and soft drinks at 861 tables that stretched for one and a quarter miles.

The evening before her wedding Diana watched the television and saw her fiancé light a beacon in Hyde Park, the first in a chain of bonfires that would be lit nationwide that night. Students from Trinity College, Cambridge, where Prince Charles had been a student, sat on the sidewalk wearing evening dress while they enjoyed a candlelit dinner and waited for the big day to begin.

There were fireworks, gun salvos, and music from massed bands and choirs. It would have been strange if Diana had slept very well with all the noise outside her window.

9

She woke early in the morning with no appetite at all. The sun was shining, so one of her worries seemed over. Diana was excited and nervous, but no more so than those around her. Her mother was the first to arrive; then came the hairdresser, the makeup artist, and the Emanuels to supervise the final fitting. To satisfy their superstition, the last stitch had to be sewn while the bride was wearing the gown.

Next came the young bridesmaids, who were to be dressed and primped for the big occasion. Diana had seven attendants. All were either Charles's relations or children of friends. The chief bridesmaid was seventeen-year-old Lady Sarah Armstrong-Jones, the daughter of Princess Margaret. She had also been bridesmaid to Diana's sister Sarah. Two of the attendants were Charles's goddaughters, thirteen-year-old India Hicks and six-year-old Catherine Cameron. Sarah Jane Gaselee, eleven, was the daughter of Charles's principal horse trainer. The youngest bridesmaid was the one Diana knew best. Diana had been Clementine Hambro's kindergarten teacher.

Diana's hair was styled as she'd always worn it. She barely needed any makeup at all. She has a peaches-and-cream complexion, and when excited (how could she not be?) she blushes naturally. Her nails were painted with a clear gloss, and then the dress was slipped over her head.

As the billows of pure ivory silk taffeta settled into place, there were oh's and ah's of approval. The silk had come from Britain's own silk farm at Lullingstone, where workers had been scouring the countryside for months for a generous supply of mulberry leaves to make the silkworms happy. Its entire output was channeled to the important task of making the princess's wedding gown.

The dress was a combination of the theatrical and romantic. It was decorated with an overlay of Carrickmacross lace. The pearl-encrusted lace, which had once belonged to Queen Mary, had been dyed a slightly lighter shade of ivory than the dress. This was the "something old"; the dress itself, of course, was new. Her mother's earrings and the Spencer tiara that held the veil in place had been borrowed from both sides of her family. A tiny blue bow was concealed in the waistband. Tucked away in the folds of the taffeta was a tiny gold horseshoe studded with diamonds for luck.

The bodice had a low-cut ruffled neckline. The full sleeves were gathered at the elbow and edged with a cascade of lace.

The silk shoes, which were almost entirely hidden from view, were nevertheless a masterpiece. A tiny heart motif was outlined by nearly 150 pearls and 500 sequins. As a special precaution against slipping, the soles were covered with the finest suede.

The bridesmaids were dressed in simplified versions of the more elegant gown of the bride. Their sashes and shoes were yellow, a color selected in memory of Prince Charles's

An official portrait of the newlyweds. Diana's ivory silk gown has a
25-foot train.

godfather Earl Mountbatten, who had recently been killed. The Mountbatten rose was also part of the bridal bouquet. Dainty white orchids and lily of the valley were framed with leaves of myrtle and veronica from bushes planted from Queen Victoria's wedding bouquet that are still growing on the Isle of Wight. All the work and planning had been worth the final pageant.

The streets had been blocked to traffic since four in the morning. Invited guests had started to fill the cathedral at nine. Two thousand six hundred fifty invitations had been issued, most to the diplomatic corps, servants of the crown, heads of industry, and local government officials. Most of the crowned heads of Europe were there, as were 160 foreign presidents and prime ministers. President Ronald Reagan was unable to attend, but his wife, First Lady Nancy Reagan, was there to represent the United States.

Diana had been given five hundred invitations to distribute among her friends and relatives. Her three former roommates were to be seated at the very front of the church, even ahead of many of the heads of state. It was a sure sign that she was having her say on arrangements. She invited some of her old schoolmates and teachers from both Riddlesworth and West Heath and all ten of the people she had worked with at the London kindergarten. Some of the staff at Althorp were delighted and surprised to receive the coveted invitations. They traveled to London by bus for the great day. Diana even remembered her old governess, whom she hadn't seen for several years. Little Patrick Robinson, whom she looked after, and his parents received one of the gilt-edged invitations. They were all waiting for her.

Four thousand police were on hand to keep order. Riot squads were at the ready. Mounted police and plainclothesmen were keeping an eye out for trouble. A helicopter hovered overhead. Marksmen were stationed on rooftops. One hundred thirty-one closed-circuit television cameras monitored every inch of the route. A special agent dressed in royal livery and armed with a .38 Smith & Wesson handgun was to ride on the back of Prince Charles's open carriage. But there was no violence in the mood of the day, only joy and happiness, contagious good humor, and spontaneous love and affection.

The carefully timed procession was five minutes late in starting to make sure the twenty-five-foot-long train was carefully folded in the cramped glass coach. Diana's father sat beside her. Because she was still a commoner, her escort was composed of mounted civil and military police; later it would be a royal guard. For twenty minutes she passed through the streets lined with cheering faces, waving hands, and clicking cameras.

The coach halted at the foot of the steps to the cathedral. A footman dressed in scarlet and gold state livery opened the door. Her father was helped out first. It was obvious that he had not entirely recovered from his stroke some months before. Next Diana stepped out. Two of her bridesmaids rushed forward to help spread the train behind her.

No one had a full view until she climbed the twenty-four red carpeted steps of St. Paul's at eleven o'clock, but four hours later, a London bridal shop claimed to have finished a simplified version of the gown. Within five hours after that copies of the dress were on sale.

The steps were lined by officers of the three services. Her father clasped her left arm in his partially paralyzed right arm. They were preceded by eleven members of the clergy wearing sumptuous red, silver, and gold vestments and were followed by her five bridesmaids and two pages. Young Edward van Cutsem, eight, and Lord Nicholas Windsor, eleven, were dressed in copies of 1863 naval uniforms.

As Diana and her father entered the west doors, the state trumpeters sounded a fanfare, and the wedding procession began. Earl Spencer leaned heavily on his daughter's arm, but this was one day he was not to miss. It took three and a half minutes to walk the full length of the aisle. "I was so nervous," she said later, "I hardly knew what I was doing."

When the clergy stepped aside, Diana caught sight of her husband-to-be for the first time. He was wearing the full dress uniform of a Royal Navy commander, with a splendid blue sash tied diagonally across his chest, signifying the distinctive Order of the Garter. Instead of one best man, the honor was shared by his two brothers, Andrew and Edward.

Prince Charles smiled at her and moved forward. "You look wonderful," he whispered.

"Wonderful for you," was her answer.

She passed her bridal bouquet to Lady Sarah while Charles took her right hand. Her father continued to stand by her side until the archbishop asked, "Who giveth this woman to be married to this man?" Her father acknowledged his position and then stepped back.

Only once did she show nervousness as she rushed her words during their vows. "I Diana Frances," she began, "take thee Philip Charles Arthur George." It should have been Charles Philip Arthur George. The error was that she had reversed the order of Charles's names. For a moment she hesitated.

This was followed by the blessing of the ring, a ring that was made out of the same piece of gold that had been used for the wedding rings of the Queen Mother, the queen, Princess Margaret, and Princess Anne. It came from a large nugget found some fifty years ago in a mine in North Wales. The last of the historic nugget had been used for Diana's ring.

Now it was Charles's turn to make a minor error, omitting a word and altering another. He said, "All thy goods with thee I share," instead of "All my worldly goods."

They were then pronounced husband and wife. Earl Spencer's son helped his father to a chair. The bride and groom were seated on stools for the rest of the ceremony. Later they were led by the archbishop into the south aisle, where they signed two registers, one for the state and the royal register kept by the lord chamberlain.

When this was completed, they returned to the center of the cathedral. Her veil was now thrown back, and everyone could see her smiling, blushing face. As they reached the dais where they had taken their vows, the princess turned and curtsied to the queen. The prince bowed to his mother. Diana's bridesmaid returned her bouquet, and the happy couple marched out of the church to the solemn strains of "Pomp and Circumstance."

The bride and the groom appeared at the west door at ten minutes after twelve just as the cathedral bells of St. Paul's rang twelve times. They were answered by other bells throughout the city. The cheers of the crowd waiting to catch a glimpse of them were deafening.

They were assisted into the open carriage that had brought Prince Charles to the church earlier that morning. The prince suggested, "Give them a wave." The princess smiled and happily obliged.

The queen and the rest of the wedding party followed five minutes later, the queen riding with Earl Spencer; Mrs. Shand Kydd with the Duke of Edinburgh; the Queen Mother with Prince Andrew; and five more carriages crammed full of royalty.

People on the streets began to surge toward Buckingham Palace. Chants of "We want Di! We want Charles!" rattled the windows. When the bride and groom and royal family appeared at the crimson-draped balcony the crowd went wild. At first Princess Diana seemed a bit overwhelmed by the greeting. By the time they were called out for their fourth appearance she seemed relaxed and able to enjoy herself. Prince Charles kissed his bride on the lips. The applause was thunderous. The world was in love with the lovers.

The official wedding pictures were taken in the Throne Room. The queen's cousin Patrick Lichfield had brought along a police whistle to keep order among the chattering royalty. Then it was time for the wedding breakfast served at two-thirty in the afternoon. One hundred eighteen guests joined them, mostly members of the immediate family rather than diplomatic guests. The wedding cake was cut by Charles with his ceremonial sword. Actually there were sixteen wedding cakes, but fifteen were unsolicited gifts.

The bride changed into her going-away outfit before emerging for their next public appearance. She looked radiant in a pale coral pink suit with a matching hat trimmed with fluttering feathers. The family tossed rose petals. Prince Andrew and Prince Edward had attached some helium-filled

Charles and Diana wave from their open carriage after the wedding ceremony at St. Paul's Cathedral.

balloons taken from the ball two nights before to the back of the royal carriage. They'd also hung on a "Just Married" sign, as if the royal pair were just like any other couple speeding off in their old car.

The train was waiting for them on Platform 12. Just before climbing aboard Diana stopped and kissed the two people who had been most involved with the planning of the day's activities, Sir "Johnnie" Johnson, comptroller to the queen, who handles her finances, and Lord Chamberlain Maclean. It was a surprising gesture and probably not what any other member of the royal family would have done, but it proved without the shadow of a doubt that Diana was going to make up some of her own rules from now on.

Broadlands was the first stop on their honeymoon journey. It was a beautiful estate surrounded by six thousand acres of grounds that was being patrolled to keep out any unwanted visitors. It was now owned by Mountbatten's grandson, Lord Romsey, a good friend and cousin of the prince. Queen Elizabeth and Prince Philip had also spent their honeymoon at Broadlands thirty-four years before.

The owners had moved out to give the bride and groom all the privacy that royal security would permit. Later, when asked the very personal question of how they'd spent the rest of their first day together, Charles admitted that for an hour or two they'd watched a video replay of their own wedding.

He tried to put his feelings into words. "We still think about it. We still can't get over what happened that day. Neither of us will ever forget the atmosphere. It was electric, I felt, and I know my wife agrees. The noise outside [at Buckingham Palace] was almost unbelievable, and I remember standing at the window trying to realize what it was like, so

Some of the members of the royal wedding group. *From l to r, first row:*
Edward van Cutsem; the Earl of Ulster; Catherine Cameron; Clementine
Hambro; Sarah Jane Gaselee; Lord Nicholas Windsor. *Second row:* King
Baudouin and Queen Fabiola of Belgium; Princess Margaret; Princess Anne;
the Queen Mother; the queen; India Hicks; Lady Sarah Armstrong-Jones;
the Honorable Mrs. Shand Kydd; Earl Spencer; Lady Sarah McCorquodale;
Neil McCorquodale; Queen Beatrix of the Netherlands; Lady Helen Windsor.
Third row: the Prince of Denmark; Queen Margrethe of Denmark; King
Olav of Norway; James and Marina Ogilvy; Captain Mark Phillips; the
Honorable Angus Ogilvy; Princess Alexandra; Prince Andrew; Viscount
Linley; the duchess of Gloucester; Prince Phillip; the duke of Gloucester;
Prince Edward; Princess Alice; the Princess of Wales; Ruth, Lady Fermoy;
the Prince of Wales; the duke of Kent (behind Lady Fermoy); the Earl
of St. Andrews (behind the Prince of Wales); the duchess of Kent; Lady
Jane Fellowes; behind her, Viscount Althorp; Robert Fellowes; Prince
Michael of Kent; Princess Michael of Kent; Princess Grace of Monaco;
Prince Albert, Hereditary Prince of Monaco; immediately below him,
Prince Claus of the Netherlands; Princess Gina and Prince Franz Josef
of Liechtenstein.

that I might be able to tell my own children. . . . It was something quite extraordinary. . . . I was quite extraordinarily proud to be British."

The day after the wedding the prince went salmon fishing, and the new princess enjoyed swimming in the heated pool. For two days they could be away from the crowds and relax. On Friday the weather turned to rain, but on Saturday, August 1, when they were to leave, it cleared. They were driven eight miles to the nearest small airport, where they boarded an antiquated but perfectly maintained propeller-driven plane for their flight to Gibraltar. The prince took over as pilot for the entire five-and-a-half-hour trip.

The fact that the royal couple was visiting a patch of British territory that Spain wanted to reclaim had caused the king and queen of Spain to refuse the invitation to Charles and Diana's wedding, but the people of Gibraltar made up with their warm welcome for any slight that might have been felt against the British crown.

The royal yacht *Britannia* had arrived in port the day before. Charles and Diana entertained Governor and Lady Jackson and a few local dignitaries on board for drinks, but later that night the *Britannia* slipped out of the harbor with no fanfare.

She is a large ship, with a crew of 277, but for the next week, in an elaborate game of cat and mouse, she was able to elude the press fleet that was sailing in and out of every possible harbor in search of her. While the reporters were scanning the Greek islands, the *Britannia* was sailing along the coast of Algeria and Tunisia. When the press gave up and started back west, the royal yacht slipped through the Strait of Messina and arrived off the coast of the Greek island of

Ithaca. Diana and Charles spent their days sunbathing and swimming and wind surfing off the side of the ship and playing deck games with the crew. In the evenings various groups of officers and crew entertained them at dinner. Their schedule was planned according to their whim of the moment, which seldom happens in a royal life.

On the twelfth day they dropped anchor at Port Said. This time they were greeted with cheering crowds and ships' sirens blaring. For two days they entertained and were entertained by President Anwar al-Sadat of Egypt and his wife Jihan. The two women instantly took a liking to each other. It was with promises that they would see each other again soon that Diana and Charles said farewell. On Saturday morning they left their floating palace and flew to Scotland to join the rest of the royal family at Balmoral.

The prince and princess agreed to one photo session if they'd be left alone later. For once the press corps took pity on them. The royal pair smiled and joked with the reporters who'd been unsuccessfully scanning the Mediterranean Sea for sight of them. After an hour of posing and snapping they left.

Charles spent a considerable time salmon fishing and shooting, two sports that don't interest Diana. She had never enjoyed riding either, so there wasn't much else for her to do but hike across the treeless fields. Granted, it is a beautiful spot, but boredom was fast setting in.

After two weeks Prince Andrew took it upon himself to invite two of her old roommates to join them. Virginia Pitman and Carolyn Pride arrived, and so did Sarah Armstrong-Jones, her eldest bridesmaid. They occasionally were able to slip away in Diana's new Ford Escort to view the countryside

The newlyweds on their honeymoon at Balmoral.

from behind the wheel and perhaps to discover come quaint shop or byway no one else knew about. But Diana began to realize her life did have limitations. Her bodyguard was never far away.

There were a few celebrations that broke the monotony, like the Braemer Royal Highland Gathering, but even here rules were to be followed. When Diana was caught whispering to Charles during the playing of the national anthem, she earned a hard stare from the queen. Her days of royal duty were about to begin.

10

Diana's greatest test was to come in Wales. Her title made her its symbolic monarch, but in the homes of socialist working-class Welsh nationalists, royalty had never been welcome. Signs were being prepared saying, "Go Home English Princess!" Threatening letters had been sent to the BBC (British Broadcasting Corporation). The royal couple was advised to cancel the trip for safety's sake, but tradition had to be maintained.

As soon as Diana appeared there was an astonishing change in sentiment. Tom Davis, reporting for the *Observer,* wrote, "Seasoned analysts of the Welsh psyche are having trouble sorting out why the Welsh have fallen so abjectly and hopelessly in love with Princess Diana. For three days and four hundred miles last week there was an astonishing sight of a whole nation having a nervous breakdown on windswept pavements. Choirs sang, harps tinkled and grown men cried."

The hostile demonstrations fell flat. The princess solved everything with her smiles. She seemed to be completely unable to tell who was for her and who against, and soon her smiles were returned.

The Prince of Wales accepted his minor rank in popularity with happy resignation. As more and more bouquets were pressed into Diana's arms, she had to ask him to help her carry them. Everyone wanted to meet her. "I'm just a collector of flowers these days," he said with a grin. "I don't have enough wives to go around."

What the people on the streets were saying was that she never seemed "posh" or "above it." She was a beautiful princess and a very human princess.

Davis again wrote, "The real key to her success must be the way she can suddenly stop smiling at the crowd and look around for no obvious reason, with the purest terror in her eyes. . . . Welsh women in particular love this air of vulnerability, and their dearest wish would be to take her home to administer many cups of tea, a mountain of well-meaning advice and an aspirin to put her right."

In spite of these moments of terror, she began to enjoy her job. Her wardrobe had been carefully selected in the Welsh colors of red and green, but no one could have predicted such cold wet weather. Diana never once complained, knowing that the people lining her route had been standing out in the rain longer than she had. She took one child's hands in her own to warm them. She seemed to have just the right small talk that sounded natural and unrestrained. She complimented one wife on having polished her husband's medals so well. The woman beamed. Probably no other "royal" would have realized that medals do require polish.

She was just beginning to enjoy her "walk-abouts" when she began to feel queasy in the morning, sometimes dizzy too. The diagnosis was that she was pregnant. Both Charles and

Diana charmed the crowds during a trip to Florence.

Diana were thrilled. They had both wanted to start raising a family right away. Diana called all of her close friends to tell them the exciting news before they read it in the papers. On November 5 the official word was given.

Several precedents were about to be set. The royal heir was to be born in the private wing of St. Mary's Hospital, not in Buckingham Palace. And Prince Charles would be the first royal father to witness the birth of his child. Dr. George Pinker, the queen's surgeon gynecologist, would be in attendance. Diana signed up for prenatal instruction to be given by nurse Betty Parsons, who has been preparing expectant mothers, over 16,500 of them, for the past thirty years. She calls them her "huff and puff classes." Fathers, even a Prince of Wales, are given lectures on what to expect and how they can be helpful.

Diana was so proud of her new condition that she started wearing loose-fitting, flowing dresses long before they were needed. She continued to attend as many public functions as she could, although she confessed to a woman in York, "Some days I feel terrible. No one told me I would feel like I do."

Again the press was being unruly, photographing every uncomfortable moment. Diana had not had the protection of Buckingham Palace the year before. This time the queen called an unprecedented conference of all representatives of the news media and asked them to take Diana's condition into consideration. She was under an unusual strain, and surely no one wanted to have their thoughtless behavior cause her to have a miscarriage. The queen explained that the poor girl couldn't even buy a packet of wine gum (candy) without becoming front-page news. One of the editors said she ought to send a servant out to fetch it. "That is the most pompous thing I've ever heard," said the queen. Diana had a powerful ally.

In the spring, when she was six months pregnant and on vacation in the Caribbean with her husband, a long-range camera caught her wearing a bikini. It was on the front pages of all the papers. The royal family was furious.

Just before dawn on Monday morning, June 21, 1982, Diana had her first labor pains. She woke her husband and dressed herself. They were driven through the deserted streets of London from Kensington Palace to the West London hospital. They arrived at 5:10, but there would still be a long wait. Dr. Pinker carefully monitored the mother's progress. He believes a birth is a natural process and should be treated as such. He rarely wears a hospital coat, merely putting on a plastic apron and a pair of boots and rolling up his sleeves for the actual delivery.

That delivery took place at three minutes after nine in the evening. The as yet unnamed young prince weighed in at seven pounds one and a half ounces. He cried lustily at birth and was handed to his mother even before the umbilical cord was cut.

The first person to hear the news was the queen, who had been waiting anxiously at Buckingham Palace. Prince Philip had been dining at Cambridge College when he was called to the phone. "It's a boy," was the happy news. Princess Margaret was at a musical show in London when the news was told to the delighted audience. Diana's mother had arrived in London for the start of the Wimbledon matches, hoping to be on hand for the birth of her royal grandchild. Johnnie Spencer was waiting at Althorp. Princess Anne was in the United States, Prince Andrew in the South Atlantic during the Falkland crisis, and Prince Edward at the Gordonstoun School. The official announcement was posted on the gates at the palace in traditional style, and the celebrations began.

Prince Charles stayed at the hospital until Diana and Baby Wales, as he was tagged, were asleep. He emerged from the hospital at eleven o'clock, grinning from ear to ear, and for once delighted to talk to the press. Standing on the steps he said, "I'm obviously relieved and delighted—sixteen hours is a long time to wait. It's rather a grown-up thing, I find— rather a shock to the system."

"How is the baby?" someone asked.

"He looks marvelous, fair, sort of blondish. He's not bad."

"Does he look like his father?"

"He has the good fortune not to."

Someone at the back of the crowd shouted, "Nice one, Charlie. Give us another one."

"Bloody hell, give us a chance," was the answer.

Charles arrived the next morning at 8:45. Then came Diana's mother and her sister Jane. They left saying, "There's a lot of happiness up there."

The queen brought a small present. Then came Earl Spencer, the proud grandfather. "It's a lovely baby."

Charles obliged the press with a further description of his son. "He's looking a bit more human this morning, and yes, Diana is recovering her strength, doing very well."

She was doing so well that they left the hospital that very afternoon. Of course, they were going home with exceptional professional helpers. Dr. Pinker and Dr. Harvey, the pediatrician, would be making daily calls, and nurse Ann Wallace, who had taken care of Princess Anne's two babies in their first few weeks, would be there to help Mother and Father take care of the new young prince.

A week later Baby Wales was given some very impressive names. He was to be known as William Arthur Philip Louis. Six godparents were chosen. There was Natali, the twenty-three-year-old Duchess of Westminster; Lady Susan Hussey; Sir Laurens van der Post, a seventy-five-year-old South African explorer and writer whom Charles had met and admired years ago; and three relatives of Charles: Constantine, former king of the Hellenes; Lord Romsey, at whose home Diana and Charles had stayed at the beginning of their honeymoon; and Charles's cousin Princess Alexandra.

Diana celebrated her own twenty-first birthday very quietly. The main event, Prince William's christening, was held on the Queen Mother's eighty-second birthday. The ceremony was conducted by the archbishop of Canterbury in the Music Room at Buckingham Palace. The prince wore the traditional christening robe of Honiton lace that had been used by generations of royal babies since 1841. He carried out his first official duty of posing for pictures with royal aplomb.

Everyone wanted to know just how much time Diana was spending with her baby. The answer: every moment she could spare from her regular duties. She has lent her name as patron or president to the Welsh National Opera, the Wales Craft Council, the Swansea Festival of Music and Arts, the Royal School of the Blind, the British Deaf Association, the Malcolm Sargent Cancer Fund for Children, Birthright (which researches the causes and prevention of birth defects), the Pre-school Playgroups Association, the Albany (a community center in South-East London), the British Red Cross Youth, the Royal College of Physicians and Surgeons of Glasgow, the

Prince William of Wales, the royal couple's first child, was born on June 21, 1982.

London City Ballet, the National Children's Orchestra, and the National Rubella Campaign. There are public functions she must attend for each of these organizations.

The trained nurse was replaced by a capable nanny, Barbara Barnes, but Diana let it be known that the job was one of a mother's helper, not a mother's stand-in. Most often it is Diana, and sometimes Prince Charles, who bathes the young prince and puts him to bed. Diana is trying to give her son a more normal life than any other heir to the throne has enjoyed.

Prince William was barely two months old when he flew with his mother and father, all on the same plane, to Balmoral. This had never been permitted before, but Diana didn't want to be separated from either her husband or her son.

In March 1983 another royal precedent was set. Prince William accompanied his parents on their six-week tour of New Zealand and Australia. His nanny was there to tend to his routine when Diana and Charles were busy, but it was obvious at William's "press conference" that Mom and Dad were the ones he delighted in being with. He tottered from one parent's knee to the other's with whoops of pleasure.

He's a bright, active little boy and has proved to be a royal handful at times. Once, when he was visiting Balmoral, he caught sight of a small button in the nursery that he hadn't noticed before. He tried it out with a whack, sending a signal directly to police headquarters in Aberdeen. After the first commotion he had caused had settled down, he had great fun repeating the process. Finally a new William-proof button was installed.

On television Prince William uttered one of his first recognizable words, "yuk." It was obvious where he'd learned this. It's one of Diana's favorite expressions. Her hair is "yuk" when it's windblown. The press is "yuk" when they pester her.

Although Prince William is right in the middle of a whole new generation of royal babies, with cousins in every direction, Diana and Charles never intended to have an only child. On February 14, Buckingham Palace announced that Diana was pregnant again and expecting her second child in September.

Once past the original stage of morning sickness, she enjoyed her role of motherhood. It meant that her schedule as a working princess was curtailed. She had more time to play with William, work on her embroidery, and plan the rearrangement of furniture at Highgrove. She put herself on a strict routine not to gain as much weight, thirty pounds, as she'd gained with William. Both she and Charles limit the rich food they eat. He runs in the morning before breakfast. Diana keeps fit with her swimming. During her pregnancy she was more radiant than ever. She wore bright colors and created a fashionable appearance wherever she went.

Again plans were made to have the baby at St. Mary's Hospital, with the same doctor, the same nurse, and the same suite. Even Prince Charles felt more relaxed, having been through the experience before.

On September 15, 1984, the formal announcement was made: "A second son was born to Diana, Princess of Wales, age twenty-three, and her husband Prince Charles, age thirty-five. The prince was in attendance. The baby weighed six pounds fourteen ounces."

At the christening of Prince Henry of Wales, the second son of Charles and Diana. *Front row, left to right:* Lady Fermoy; the Queen Mother; Prince William (immediate foreground); the queen; Princess Diana holding Prince Henry; Prince Charles; the Honorable Mrs. Shand Kydd. *Back row, left to right:* Lady Sarah Armstrong-Jones; Bryan Organ; Gerald Ward; Prince Andrew; Prince Phillip; Lord Spencer; Lady Cece Vestey; and Mrs. William Bartholomew.

The news was greeted by cheers from the crowd that had stood outside the hospital since the princess's arrival early that morning. It was also heralded by a forty-one-gun salute from troops in Hyde Park. The newest prince, named Henry Charles Albert David, will be known as Prince Henry of Wales, if he can escape the nickname of Harry already bestowed by his doting public. He is third in the line of royal succession after his father and brother.

Prince Henry immediately took his place in the close family group and, in spite of Diana's protests, was royally spoiled on his first Christmas.

Christmas is always spent at Windsor Castle. The queen is the first to arrive. About thirty members of the family take part, each family unit having its own suite of rooms. The Red Drawing Room is changed into a display area for all the treats and surprises wrapped in tissue and foil. Presents tend to be practical—lamps, a car robe, books or ties, even a doormat, perhaps some new piece of sporting equipment—but there's plenty of excitement and anticipation.

The furniture and rugs are removed from the room, and a long trestle table is set up and divided into sections. The first is piled with presents for the queen, the next for Prince Philip, then the Queen Mother, and so on down to the youngest of the royal family, Prince Henry.

The presents are opened at teatime on Christmas Eve. The doors are shut. The staff is not allowed to peek, but there are plenty of shrieks of "Look what I got!" to be heard. In the evening when the young children are asleep, the royal family frequently turn to their favorite parlor game, Charades. The results are often hilarious. Prince Charles grew up with these large family get-togethers, but it is a new experience for Diana.

On Christmas morning each branch of the family stay together in their own private rooms for their own celebration. The day starts with an early communion service for the adults. Again they attend church at 11:15. Here the children join their parents for carol singing. At one o'clock Queen Elizabeth delivers her traditional Christmas television broadcast from the castle.

Lunch is served in the State Dining Room with traditional roast turkey and plum pudding. It is totally private. There are paper hats and snappers and a fun-filled, not too dignified time is had by all. On the next weekday, known in England as Boxing Day, most of the men in the royal family take part in a shoot. New Year's is always celebrated at Sandringham, familiar ground for Diana.

She has learned that there are traditions to be followed. A friend of Prince Charles predicted before the wedding, "Whoever Charles marries will have to accept the idea of spending every summer in Scotland at Balmoral and every winter at Sandringham, plodding up and down hills in the foulest of weather, stalking animals, or standing knee deep in the icy waters of a salmon river. Charles is a traditional man and he will not change."

But in small ways he has changed. For one thing, he no longer hunts. Diana has had a hand in selecting his wardrobe and she has persuaded him to have his hair cut by her hairdresser. He's been known to attend a rock concert where most of the audience was a wave of screaming teens. The future king of England is not a henpecked husband, however. He is a husband very much in love. Diana returns that affection and respect.

He is a great support to her on their trips. In the summer of 1985 they traveled to Italy. They had a private audience with the pope, although Queen Elizabeth prohibited the royal couple from attending a Mass. She did not think it proper for a future head of the Church of England to attend a Roman Catholic service.

The same year they planned to visit Australia again and then the United States. This time their two young sons would be left at home, but Diana insisted that their trip be cut short. She had no intention of being separated from her family for the months the Queen Mother was expected to be apart from hers during the first part of her reign.

Charles's grandmother is very understanding and has often given Diana good advice. For instance, "Forget yesterday and tomorrow when you are meeting people. Today is the most important day and the person to whom you are talking is the most important person."

Queen Mary's words to a relative complaining of fatigue were, "Stuff and nonsense. You are a member of the British royal family, and WE are never tired."

Diana's very special appeal to the young has revitalized the role of the monarchy. She has been able to combine independence and respect for her position. She has done a great deal to bring back the concept of the importance of family life.

"She is also the best advertisement for Britain since the Beatles," said Dick Guttman, a member of a prominent public relations firm. "England is always in danger of falling back into the nineteenth century in people's perceptions. They had the Beatles and the fashions of Mary Quant and Carnaby Street that gave the country a great shot in the 60s. Then it was over. I think that Princess Diana provides the country with something they couldn't have manufactured."

Diana and Charles talking with Pope John Paul II during their tour of Italy.

With apologies to Winston Churchill, one journalist states that "Seldom in the course of human endeavor, have so many owed so much to one unofficially unemployed mother of two." As a fashion plate she has done "incredible things for British fashion and its exports."

Her insistence on wearing only British designed clothes has been greeted with applause. In 1981 she wore a sweater decorated with cute little sheep. The manufacturer has now sold one million dollars worth of copies. Patterned stockings, low-heeled shoes, hats—without Diana those styles would never have made headlines.

Tourists are flocking to England, not just because they think they'll be lucky enough to cross paths with the glamorous princess, but to see the sights they are reading about in magazines and newspapers and are seeing on TV.

Her short trip to the United States in November 1985 was planned naturally as a demonstration of goodwill and friendship between the two countries, but it was also used as an outright promotion of British industry. Charles and Diana came ostensibly for the opening of Washington's National Gallery of Art exhibit "The Treasure Houses of Britain: Five Hundred Years of Private Patronage and Art Collecting." More than seven hundred works of art from some two hundred of the most splendid British country homes were assembled for the showing. Elegant furniture, priceless paintings, books, and tapestries were all seen for the first time in this country. But what most Americans wanted to see was the princess in person.

Invitations to the social events were so sought after that the offices of President and Mrs. Reagan were flooded with requests that obviously could not be filled.

The royal couple were house guests of the British ambassador while in Washington. They were entertained lavishly both at the White House and the British Embassy.

On Veterans Day, Charles laid a wreath at Arlington National Cemetery while Diana was taken on a tour of a Washington home for the aged. She thrilled the residents with her warm, natural, spontaneous ability to put people at ease.

Crowds viewed the couple when they attended church services at the Washington Cathedral and when they paid a visit to a shopping mall in nearby Springfield, Virginia. J. C. Penney Company was participating in a mammoth promotion of merchandise from the British Isles. Everything featured, from the Rolls Royce balanced on four Wedgewood teacups to the women's and men's fashions, were English products.

President Reagan and the First Lady entertaining the Prince and Princess of Wales in the West Hall of the White House.

Such a crass commercial appearance horrified some of the more conservative British subjects, but Charles quite frankly gave his own views on a TV program preceding their trip. "Creating a positive atmosphere toward Britain is one of the major functions of the royals. I would like to hope that maybe through trying to engender that sort of awareness and interest . . . that other things will follow, like increased trade and export opportunities. This is an area which, I feel, hasn't been concentrated on enough. It is very difficult for us to say how much can be achieved, but it's amazing, sometimes, what can be achieved through goodwill."

Their goodwill continued to spread when they flew to Palm Beach, Florida. Charles displayed his expert playing form on the polo field during a benefit game that helped raise money for one of Charles's pet causes, the United World colleges. That evening after the match Charles and Diana attended a dinner dance at the fashionable Breakers Hotel. Those who had donated $25,000 or more to the scholarship fund of the colleges in the federation had a chance to dance the night away with the royal couple.

The press went out of its mind trying to cover every moment of their visit. As they headed home aboard the royal plane there was no doubt that Diana had charmed the American public.

On March 19, 1986, the press focused on the announcement of Prince Andrew's engagement to a charming redhead, Sarah Ferguson. "Fergie" is a good friend of Diana's, who, it is said, thoroughly enjoyed playing royal matchmaker for the couple.

As Diana matures, her role will grow as will her title. Her Royal Highness will undoubtedly be addressed one day as "Your Majesty."

INDEX